# Mills & Boon
# Best Seller Romance

A chance to read and collect some of the best-loved novels from Mills & Boon—the world's largest publisher of romantic fiction.

Every month, four titles by favourite Mills & Boon authors will be re-published in the *Best Seller Romance* series.

A list of other titles in the *Best Seller Romance* series can be found at the end of this book.

# Anne Mather

# LORD OF ZARACUS

MILLS & BOON LIMITED
LONDON · TORONTO

*All the characters in this book have no existence outside the imagination of the Author, and have no relation whatsoever to anyone bearing the same name or names. They are not even distantly inspired by any individual known or unknown to the Author, and all the incidents are pure invention.*

*The text of this publication or any part thereof may not be reproduced or transmitted in any form or by any means, electronic or mechanical, including photocopying, recording, storage in an information retrieval system, or otherwise, without the written permission of the publisher.*

*This book is sold subject to the condition that it shall not, by way of trade or otherwise, be lent, resold, hired out or otherwise circulated without the prior consent of the publisher in any form of binding or cover other than that in which it is published and without a similar condition including this condition being imposed on the subsequent purchaser.*

First published 1970
Australian copyright 1981
Philippine copyright 1981
This edition 1981

© Anne Mather 1970

ISBN 0 263 73690 3

Set in Linotype Baskerville 10 on 12 pt.

*Made and printed in Great Britain by
Richard Clay (The Chaucer Press) Ltd,
Bungay, Suffolk*

# CHAPTER ONE

SINCE leaving the main highway, seventy-five miles south-west of Veracruz, the road had deteriorated into a series of ruts and pot-holes, thickly covered with fine dust, that was swept up by the passage of the Land-Rover and almost choked its occupants. Carolyn, who had had such high hopes when she left London two days ago, felt as though any minute she might be shaken out on to the roadside, and she held on desperately, trying not to look as uncomfortable as she felt. Hot and sticky, her clothes clinging to her, she felt much different from the smoothly elegant young female who had boarded the Boeing in London, and she wondered, not for the first time, whether she had made a terrible mistake in coming. But then she remembered how delighted her father had been that she should be taking an interest in his archaeological explorations, and banished the traitorous thought. After all, life in England was becoming very boring, and Alaistair Kendrew's attentions were beginning to annoy her.

She wiped her hands on a paper tissue and the driver of the Land-Rover glanced her way sympathetically.

'Not far now,' he remarked, raising her spirits a little.

Carolyn sighed. 'Thank goodness!' Then she smiled,

and the bluff good-natured Scot, Anderson, felt the usual twinges of admiration that Carolyn's appearance always aroused in him. He wondered whether her presence at the dig would cause more problems than even Professor Madison imagined.

'How is my father?' she asked now, trying to forget the soreness of her rear end.

'Oh, Maddie's okay.' Professor Madison was known to all his closest associates as 'Maddie'. 'Naturally he's looking forward to your visit. I think he's afraid that you might find things rather different from your imaginings, though.' Bill Anderson swung the wheel, narrowly avoiding a solitary cyclist as the tyres screamed round the rim of a small crater. He grinned at Carolyn's expression. 'Don't be alarmed. I haven't killed anybody yet.'

Carolyn fanned herself with her handkerchief and gave her attention to the lushness of the vegetation as the Land-Rover began the descent down a small gorge into a huge valley, bright with flame trees and other exotic plants. Running below them, along the floor of the valley, a narrow river surged coolly, and Carolyn longed to be able to soak her handkerchief in its icy depths. There seemed an abundance of trees and foliage, and the heat was quite different from the kind of temperate climate she had expected.

'What is the name of this place?' she asked, brushing back her long straight hair with a careless hand. Thick and silky, and the colour of honey, it caught Anderson's eye, and he felt the faint stirrings of attraction again.

'Oh—Zaracus,' he answered, gathering his thoughts with some difficulty. 'The valley belongs to Don Carlos

Fernandez Monterra d'Alvarez. He has a coffee plantation, but of course a manager attends to the estate. He spends much of his time elsewhere.'

'I see. And this find my father is excavating—it is in the valley, also?'

'That's right. Your father was interested in the reports made by a man called Guivas who spent many months here two years ago, investigating the possible whereabouts of another Zapotec city. As you may know, this country was overrun with various civilizations before the Spaniards came, and different parts bear witness to different civilisations, religions, cultures; you know the sort of thing. We even went so far as to visit Yucatan where the Mayan ruins were found not long ago. It's quite fantastic really, seeing these pure white pyramids rising out of the steaming jungles of Yucatan. It's all there, cities with temples and pyramids and tombs.'

Carolyn's eyes twinkled. 'You're really hooked on this kind of thing, aren't you, Bill?'

Anderson grinned. 'I guess I am. But if you'd been there, in that massive pyramid, and seen the throne of the Mayans, built to look like a jaguar, painted red and studded with jade, and knew for a fact that it was at least fourteen or fifteen hundred years old, you'd have been impressed, just as we were. That's why I'm hooked. I want to know how they built their cities, why they made them in a certain way, these ancient Aztec tribes.'

Carolyn was interested in spite of herself. 'Still,' she said, 'I didn't realise Dad was so far south when I agreed to come out. I always imagined Mexico had a pretty temperate climate.'

'So it has, in parts. Mexico City, for example, but it's

so high up you practically pant if you do anything remotely energetic.'

Carolyn chuckled. 'At least we're not short of oxygen here.'

The valley was opening out before her eyes now, and she could distinguish the regimented lines of the coffee-bean plantation, and banana trees. The closely packed trees and foliage looked as though one might be able to walk on them looking down from this height, while the small villages set higher up from the valley floor were merely brown roofs visible among the trees. The colours and scents were an assault on the senses, while the sky above was a brilliant blue as the sun sank a little lower as the day wore on. Now and then they came upon a couple of Mexicans driving small herds of cattle indiscriminately along the highway, for all the world as though they owned that particular stretch of road. Carolyn lit a cigarette, and thought that she was flattering the mud stretch by calling it a highway, or a road.

Her royal blue crimplene slack suit, which had looked so good in London, was beginning to feel like a second skin, and she wished she had thought to change into something cooler in Veracruz. She flicked out her compact and studied her reflection, taking a paper tissue and wiping the damp make-up from her face. Her complexion, already tanned after a holiday in the south of France, required little make-up, but she experimented with various face and skin creams, and in consequence felt awfully greasy. Her eyes, wide spaced and slightly slanted, were a remarkable shade of green, while her nose was small above a mouth that was generous in proportion. She knew she was very attractive, having experienced the usual compliments men made to girls they pursued, but she was completely without conceit and treated her looks as something she was fortunate enough to possess but not exactly responsible for.

Bill Anderson watched her surreptitiously, and Carolyn, aware of his scrutiny, put away the compact and concentrated again on the ever-changing scenery. It appeared an enormous valley, stretches of it out of sight of the road as it descended to floor level. Rocky promontories towered overhead, supporting cactus plants which stood out like sentinels against the skyline. The pass they had negotiated seemed to be the only access to the valley, and Carolyn said:

'Doesn't this Don Carlos whatever his name is find travelling rather arduous from this isolated place?'

Anderson crossed a narrow wooden bridge across the river which had broadened at this point and then shrugged. 'He doesn't use the road very often,' he said. 'He has a helicopter, and uses that to reach Oaxaca. He's a very go-ahead fellow, not at all what you'd expect to find in the heart of the Mexican bush.'

'He must be,' remarked Carolyn, sardonically. 'What a pity he didn't suggest loaning you his helicopter to collect me!'

'He doesn't know you are coming,' replied Anderson, frowning. 'Your father thought it best to spring it on him. He's very—oh, I don't know what you'd call him—maybe, feudal, is the right word. At any rate, I don't think the idea of a woman joining a group of males on a dig, even if her father is in charge of the expedition, would appeal to him at all. Conditions are pretty primitive, when all's said and done, and quite frankly I was amazed when Maddie said you were coming.'

Carolyn smiled. 'As you know my father so well, Bill, it must be painfully apparent to you that there are times when my father can be quite blissfully unaware of his surroundings, and on these digs I think this situation occurs. Besides, it was my idea to come, not his, and, poor darling, I don't think it would occur to him to refuse me.'

Bill Anderson thought there might be a lot of truth in that. Professor Madison spoiled his youngest daughter abominably. Her two older sisters, both in their teens when she was born, had always treated her in like manner, and as their mother had died soon after Carolyn's birth, Carolyn had been brought up by a procession of nannies, all of whom had doted on her. In consequence, she might have become a little spoiled, but her nature was so charming, she found it incredibly easy to get her own way. Professor Madison seemed unable to deny her anything, and although Anderson thought he must know that Carolyn was only coming out to Mexico to find some new kind of thrill with which to relieve her boredom he still allowed her to come. Carolyn looked at him, seeing the conflicting emotions on his face, and said with acute perspicacity:

'You're thinking Dad ought to have put his foot down and made me stay at home, aren't you?'

Bill's ruddy face was scarlet. 'It's nothing to do with me,' he mumbled, awkwardly.

'Isn't it? Perhaps not. Oh, Bill, you think I've only come for kicks, don't you?'

'Well, haven't you?'

'No. I wanted to be with Dad, really I did. If only he would let me take a job, do something useful, it would be different. As it is, I spend my days either lying in bed or at some party or race-track or casino. Heavens, I'm only twenty-two, and I don't really know of anything I particularly can look forward to.'

Bill Anderson looked thoughtful. 'I'm sorry, Carolyn,' he said, his smile repentant. 'But, please, when you get here, remember we're in the heart of a country of mainly Spanish descent, where the conventions still matter.'

Carolyn slanted her eyes at him. 'What you mean is: don't go around in tight slacks and low-cut dresses, don't you?'

Bill chuckled. 'Yes, you've said it,' he said.

'Are they all terribly conservative?'

'Terribly. At least Don Carlos is, so far as his women are concerned.'

Carolyn's eyes widened. 'His *women*!' she echoed. 'How many women does he have?'

Bill grinned. 'Oh, nothing like that, love. Perish the thought. No, he has two sisters, and then of course there is his fiancée, Louisa Morelos.'

'I see.' Carolyn grimaced. 'Well, don't worry, William. I'll be the soul of virtue!'

Bill couldn't imagine Carolyn in that role, but he hid his doubts and said: 'Well, we're almost there. We turn off here, go through this belt of trees, and then you'll see the encampment.'

Carolyn's eyes twinkled. 'Encampment! Heavens, we sound like gypsies.'

'We are, in a way. At any rate, we sleep in tents, and cook in the open most days.'

Carolyn felt those awful twinges of apprehension. 'Sounds primitive,' she murmured, and thought longingly of a shower.

The belt of trees that Bill had mentioned seemed, to Carolyn, like a closely confined piece of jungle. The track, overhung with flowering shrubs and undergrowth, was practically non-existent in places where the rain had combined with the sultry heat to cultivate thick creepers that hid the track from view. She thought it would be a terrible place to lose oneself at night. Beneath the trees the air seemed more humid than ever, and she was glad when the bright sunlight ahead of them heralded the end of the forest.

They emerged into comparatively open country, and now Carolyn could see the moderately large encampment of tents, several jeeps parked alongside, while a delicious smell of cooking made her realise suddenly that she was hungry.

'Home, sweet home,' said Bill, with some satisfaction, and Carolyn said:

'I hope there's plenty of water. I'm *dying* to rinse this awful dust off me!'

Bill gave her a sidelong glance. 'Well, there are showering facilities,' he remarked, slowly. 'But I think you might find it a little different from what you're used to.'

Carolyn spread wide her hands, stretching. 'The way I feel at the moment, I could strip off and dive into the stream,' she exclaimed. 'But it will be nice to see Dad again. And I won't make too many complaints, I promise.'

Bill brought the Land-Rover bumping across the grassy stretch to where the encampment began. Now that they were closer, Carolyn could see a definite pattern in the layout of the site. Tents, obviously used for sleeping, were grouped at one side, while the cooking and kitchen departments were housed in open-sided marquee-type dwellings. Toilet facilities were not apparently visible, and Carolyn smiled to herself with some derision. Bill had certainly been right to warn her. But she was no defeatist, and she thrust her doubts aside, and as Bill sounded his horn loudly to herald their arrival, she smiled cheerfully, and slid out of the vehicle to greet her father, who came out of one of the tents at the far side of the site, carrying his spectacles, an eye-shield pushed up his forehead. A tall, broad man with greying hair, he looked dear and lovable, and Carolyn forgot all her misgivings and sped across the dusty grass to fling her arms round him exuberantly.

Bill looked on tolerantly, while several other members of the group emerged to find out what was going on. They looked at Carolyn with some indulgence; most of them knew her, and as the majority of the party were in their forties and fifties, the sight of a pretty girl after three months in the bush was a welcome sight.

Carolyn drew back from her father, and he smiled warmly. 'Good to see you, my dear,' he said, looking at her with evident satisfaction. 'You are certainly a sight for sore eyes! Did you have a good journey?'

'So-so! It was okay until we reached Veracruz. What a terrible road we had to negotiate to get here! I thought I was going to split in two!'

Professor Madison laughed. 'Not you. You're not made of glass. You know I had my doubts earlier today, knowing what conditions are like here, but I really think it might be the best thing I've ever done for you. After all, you've been coddled long enough. It's time you learned a little about the other side of the coin. Besides, you may find it interesting.' He glanced around. 'You remember Donald, don't you?' he went on, nodding to the men who were approaching; 'and Lester, and Tom Revie.'

Carolyn nodded, and greeted the other men. There were seven or eight more on the fringes of the group who she knew less well, but she expected she would soon be familiar with all of them. She wondered what she would do, how she would fill her days, and then decided she would not think ahead, but just take every day as it came.

One of the men produced a tray of coffee, and Carolyn sat in a canvas chair, drank the coffee, smoked a cigarette, and thought things might not be so bad after all.

Her father was really pleased to see her, and they had so much to say to one another. The pride with which he introduced her to all the members of his team banished all traitorous thoughts from her mind, and she determined to show him how easily she could adapt herself to her new surroundings. At least her experiences, whatever they might turn out to be, would provide her with endless topics of conversation when she eventually returned to London.

As it was getting quite late, the men had finished their work for the day, and were quite prepared to sit around, drinking beers and smoking, and joining in the general conversation. Really, thought Carolyn, were it not for the shortage of women, they might be a group of people anywhere indulging in pre-dinner chatter.

She looked curiously at the men. Of the younger ones, she liked Bill Anderson and David Laurence best. They were both in their late twenties and unmarried. Simon Dean was young too, but as he had a wife somewhere in the background Carolyn refused to take his advances seriously. She considered him weak and self-indulgent, and felt sorry for the unfortunate Mrs. Dean wherever she might be. The older men were easier to know and easier to get along with. Donald Graham and Tom Revie she had known for a long time, and usually accompanied the professor everywhere. Young and old alike they had something in common, she decided; a love of the outdoor life, discovering ancient relics, and brown, sunburnt complexions. Dressed in open-necked shirts and either cream denims or shorts, they looked cool and relaxed, and Carolyn wished she felt the same. That was the trouble with men, she thought, they didn't seem to realise that what a woman wanted most after a journey like she had experienced was a cool shower, and a change of clothes.

Eventually, her father rose to his feet. 'Well, time's getting on,' he said, 'and I expect you'd like a shower and a change of clothes before dinner, wouldn't you, Carolyn?'

Carolyn smiled. 'I thought you'd never guess,' she said.

The professor put an arm across her shoulders. 'I'm sorry. But you've no idea how delightful it is, hearing news of England first hand. After all, the papers we get here are a week old before we read them.'

Carolyn rose also, and said: 'Where am I to sleep, then?'

Professor Madison led her across the grassy stretch to where several tents were grouped. He lifted the flap of one and said: 'This has been allotted to you, my dear, and I'm just next door. It looks spartan, but it's quite comfortable really. These air-beds are remarkably comfortable.'

Carolyn stepped inside. As her father had said, it did look spartan, the bare earth partly covered by a cotton rug beside a low camp bed. Near by was a rough wood table, and a chair, and a polythene erection served as a wardrobe. Electricity was supplied from their own generator, her father explained, which was an extension of the one owned by Don Carlos, the owner of the valley.

'I expect Bill told you about Don Carlos, didn't he?' went on the professor, smiling and nodding as two Mexicans came in carrying Carolyn's cases and boxes.

'He did mention him,' agreed Carolyn, sitting on the bed to test it. 'Sounds quite a character, by all accounts. Tell me,' she stood up, rubbing the seat of her pants, 'who supplies all this equipment?'

'We do. Lord, Carolyn, how many cases have you brought? You must have paid out a fortune in excess baggage!'

Carolyn grimaced. 'I did rather,' she nodded. 'But, darling, I couldn't come all this way, into a climate like this, without having at least two changes of clothes for every day.'

'Every day of the time you'll be here, by the looks of things,' remarked Professor Madison, dryly. 'And what's that? *A record player?*'

'Of course. Heavens, I had to provide myself with some entertainment! Besides, it will be fun in the evenings, if we can dance or something——'

'Dance!' Her father stared at her. 'Now look here, Carolyn, let's get one or two things straight first of all: to begin with, as you are the only woman in a camp of over twenty men, including the Indian helpers, of course, I want you to behave yourself. How on earth could you conduct a dance here, with every man on the site competing for your favours? No, Carolyn, that is definitely out. And another thing, I know you're used to running wild back in London, but here, in Zaracus, things are very different, and I want you to act with some degree of decorum, and finally, I do not wish you to get involved *in any way* with any of the men on the site. No'—as Carolyn would have protested—'nobody! Is that understood?'

Carolyn's cheeks were red. 'I don't know what you mean,' she exclaimed hotly. 'Heavens, you're acting as though I was the original Mata Hari, or something! I've never given you any reason to speak to me like that! I didn't come here to disrupt the expedition, I came to see you, to be with you. Now you're making me wish I'd never come!'

'Oh, Carolyn, that was not my intention, although I must admit that when I saw you arriving I had some uncertainty as to the wiseness of such an intrusion. But you're here now, and I want you to feel at home and get completely acclimatised before you meet Don Carlos. Bill may have told you that he does not know of your arrival. Needless to say, I expect a little antipathy on his part; after all, he is of Spanish descent, and they do not treat their women as equals. Certainly not as equals in an adventure of this kind. It is fortunate that he is away at the moment, which will give you the opportunity to settle in before he discovers your presence here.'

'Oh heavens!' Carolyn raised her dark eyebrows in exasperation. 'What does it matter what he thinks? He's not in charge of the expedition, you are! How can he dictate what you do?'

'Carolyn, this is Mexico, not England, and this valley belongs to Don Carlos. In the eyes of the Mexicans, he is the lord of Zaracus, and as such, his word is law! We rely a great deal on his assistance; he supplies us with the very necessary help we need for much of the labouring involved in this dig. Should he refuse us the labour, or even order us to leave the valley, we should be sunk. Surely you can see the position I am in.'

'Well, I think it all sounds positively feudal, like Bill said,' retorted Carolyn, frowning. 'But all right, Dad. We'll play it your way. Just don't expect too much all at once, will you?'

The professor laughed. 'No, I won't do that,' he said. 'Now come along, and I'll show you where the shower is. It's rather primitive, too, but no doubt it will serve the purpose.'

The shower was accommodated in a wooden shed, which Carolyn supposed was an improvement on the canvas tents. It comprised quite simply an overhead tank which was filled with rainwater, and sprayed an icy scattering of water when the catch was released. The professor laughed at Carolyn's expression, and then left her to her ablutions.

Carolyn stripped off her clothes, thrusting them carelessly into the bag she had brought with her. She laid a huge orange bath towel and her clean change of clothes over two hooks which protruded from the wooden walls. She released the plug and almost screamed with shock as the icy water fell on to her overheated body. But after a few moments the spray became quite enjoyable, and she rinsed all the dust and perspiration from her skin with appreciation. After the exhausting day she had experienced it was wonderful to feel clean and cool again, and it was amazing how her doubts and anxieties fell away with the advent of this feeling of well-being. She was about to turn off the water when looking down she saw an enormous beetle crawling across the muddy floor at her feet.

Ordinarily, she would have behaved quite sensibly and stepped out of its way, but in her still overstimulated condition it seemed the last straw. Panic overriding all her natural inhibitions she let out a sharp cry, and grabbed at the orange towel desperately. Winding it unceremoniously around her, she thrust open the door, almost falling out in her haste, and then found herself grasped roughly by a man who had narrowly avoided being hit by the carelessly opened door.

Carolyn struggled wildly, almost dislodging the indifferently fastened towel, as she looked up into the man's face. There was no doubt that he was one of the Mexicans with his darkly tanned skin and dark eyes, and she did not care just then who he was. She wanted to be free, to get as far away from that revolting insect, if such a huge thing could be called an insect, as possible.

'Let me go!' she commanded, angrily. *'Let me go!'*

'Calm yourself,' said the man, coldly, but Carolyn did not notice that he had spoken in English.

'I won't calm myself,' she exclaimed, furiously.

'Excuse me!' The sarcasm in the man's voice was lost on Carolyn, as he stepped past her and secured the catch of the tank, thus preventing the remains of its contents from being lost. Carolyn had forgotten to turn it off in her haste. Then he looked back at her and Carolyn gathered the towel closer about her, as she became aware of the scarcity of her attire. Her damp hair was in disorder about her shoulders, and for the first time in her life she felt unable to cope with the situation. She realised she must appear very foolish and her anger overrode her common decency.

'How you—you people can live in such appalling circumstances is beyond me!' she exploded. 'Like—like *animals*! Do you realise I could have been eaten alive by the bugs in that ghastly hell-hole!'

The man's eyes grew colder if that was humanly possible, and for the first time Carolyn became aware of a kind of hauteur about him, and felt the first twinges of apprehension. The man was tall, much taller than most of the Mexicans she had seen since her arrival, with a lean, hard body. His features were lean also, and if not handsome he possessed a compellingly attractive countenance. His hair was thick and black as pitch, and grew rather low on his tanned neck. Dressed in a loose white shirt, and stained, cream cotton trousers who else could he be than one of the labourers?

Then, all at once, her father was there, with Donald Graham, looking hot and flustered, his expression one of annoyance when he looked at Carolyn.

'Don Carlos,' he was saying with some humility. 'Whatever is going on here? Carolyn?'

*Don Carlos!* Carolyn's stomach plunged. It couldn't be true! This man, dressed like one of his own labourers, could not be the lord of Zaracus!

But he was, of course, and now Carolyn knew why her father was looking so angry. Hadn't he only been telling her half an hour ago that their being in the valley relied on Don Carlos's permission? But he had also said that Don Carlos was away so surely she could be forgiven for mistaking his identity. But even so, a small voice argued inside her, she had been rude, very rude, and there was no excuse for that, no matter who he was. After all, she was a visitor to his country, and as such ought to act with politeness. What had her father said? With some degree of decorum! That was it, well, she had failed, abysmally, and heaven knew what was going to happen now.

'I'm afraid this—er—young lady seems to have encountered some difficulty while she was taking a shower,' Don Carlos was saying, smoothly. 'Unfortunately, I have not the knowledge of her name, or of the reason she is here.' His eyes narrowed slightly as he looked at Professor Madison. 'I gather you know the young lady.'

His accent was effortless, and Carolyn chided herself for not realising that he was no uneducated native from the bush.

Professor Madison's face was bright red. 'I'm sorry, Don Carlos, but I feel this is neither the time nor the place to introduce you to my daughter. Carolyn, I would suggest you find your clothes and go to your tent and put them on—*at once*!'

Carolyn immediately felt as though she had been reduced to about five years old, and it took the greatest amount of courage to open the shower door and retrieve her bag and stuff her clean clothes inside it. As she did so she saw the crushed bug on the floor. Obviously someone had placed their foot firmly on it, preventing any further intrusion on its part. And only one person could have had the chance to do that.

She straightened and emerged from the hut, passing the small group of men without a word, although she allowed herself one glance at Don Carlos. Her eyes met his dark enigmatic ones for one moment, and she felt a surge of fury. She was sure she could see a faint glimmer of sardonic amusement in their depths, and gathering up the ends of the orange towel she made as distinguished an exit as she could.

## CHAPTER TWO

CAROLYN was dressed in a slim-fitting pale blue shift of tricel velvet, her hair combed smooth and caught up in a knot on top of her head when her father finally came to find her. He entered her tent looking dark-browed and angry, and Carolyn felt all her earlier trepidation materialise again.

'All right, all right,' she said, lighting a cigarette before he could say anything. 'I'm sorry if I upset your Señor d'Alvarez, or whatever his name is!'

Professor Madison's mouth was hard. 'And I suppose you think that is all that is necessary,' he said, with contempt. 'My dear Carolyn, you simply can't go around in this country acting so carelessly! I heard what you said—that the Mexicans lived like savages—and quite frankly it appalled me. If you felt like this, why on earth did you come?'

Carolyn lifted her slim shoulders helplessly. 'Oh, honestly, Dad, it wasn't like that at all. Surely, you don't imagine I walked out of the shower and attacked the man!'

'Well, what did happen?'

'Didn't *Don Carlos* enlighten you?' Her tone was sarcastic.

'Some. Obviously, as a gentleman he forbore to quote me all the distasteful details.'

'Obviously.'

'So go on. What did happen?'

Carolyn sighed, and drew on her cigarette deeply. 'Well, I was having a shower, as you know, when this enormous—beetle, I suppose you would call it, came crawling across the floor like some monstrous reincarnation of a cockroach. Naturally, I was startled, to put it mildly. I think I just grabbed the towel, and dashed out, and of course, this man—Don Carlos—was outside. Well, I practically fell into his arms, and I guess I just vent my fear and anger on him.' She flushed. 'I didn't even mean what I said. I just wanted to lash out at somebody, and he—was there,' she finished lamely.

'I see.' Her father drew out his pipe. 'And I suppose you realise that by—lashing out, as you put it, you jeopardised the security of all of us here!'

'I wasn't to know he was who he turned out to be,' protested Carolyn. 'Good lord, you had told me he was away. Besides, he doesn't dress like a—like an overlord, or anything. He—he looked like one of the Mexicans I've seen helping around the camp.'

'Don Carlos Fernandez Monterra d'Alvarez doesn't have to *look* like anything; he just *is*! As you get to know him better—or perhaps I should say, *if* you get to know him better, you will realise that he emanates authority, with every gesture, every movement he makes. Besides, he is well liked by everyone, and in short, treats his workers with real consideration. That is why it is insufferable that you should treat him so abominably. Can't you see that by treating him like that, no matter who you thought he was, you have insulted *him*, his authority, if you like. He would not care for you to speak to his lowliest peasant as you spoke to him!'

'Oh, Dad!' Carolyn studied the glowing tip of her cigarette. It was getting dark in the tent, and the professor leaned across to switch on the table lamp by the bed.

Her father chewed his pipe reflectively, and looked at Carolyn intently. 'I—I may have to ask you to return to England,' he began.

She swung round. 'You may *what*!'

'I'm sure you heard every word I said, Carolyn.'

'But why? Dad, honestly, isn't this getting a bit ridiculous? I mean, all right, I was rude, but heavens, the conditions are primitive. All right, I shouldn't have said what I did, and if it makes you any happier, I'll apologise to your *Don Carlos*——'

'That you most certainly will do, whatever happens,' ground out her father. 'It appears to me, Carolyn, that the freedom and lack of authority you have experienced in London have changed you from a decent, thoughtful child, into a sharp-tongued young woman, without much thought for anyone but herself.'

'*Dad!*' Carolyn sounded hurt.

'Well, it's true, Carolyn. I suppose I have been rather careless in my duties as your father, but I always thought you were well-cared for. I do not care for too much of this modern idea of plain speaking.'

Carolyn stubbed out her cigarette. 'I think it's all been taken far too seriously. I was tired and frightened. I should think anyone in my position, any woman that is, would have done the same.'

'That is a matter of opinion. Certainly, no one in Don Carlos's sphere would have accused him of being an *animal*!'

'Oh, for goodness sake! What do you want me to

say? Where is the man, and I'll apologise?'

'He's gone back to his home.'

'Why did he come, anyway?'

'To let me know he had returned. He has been in Acapulco for the last three weeks, and only returned this morning. It is unfortunate he had to be apprised of your arrival in such a manner. As it is, I have yet to explain that I agreed for you to come. I knew your presence here would not please him. After all, it is true, digs of this kind are not suitable places for young women alone. Usually, if any women are taken along, there are at least two or three of them in the party. I really feel I have made a mistake, Carolyn.'

Carolyn's eyes widened. 'You're not going to make me go back?' She clasped her hands. 'Oh, please, don't do that! At least, give me a chance to show that I am as capable as anyone else of adapting myself to my surroundings. It's all been a storm in a tea-cup, so couldn't we forget it?' Her eyes were appealing.

Professor Madison shrugged his heavy shoulders, and studied his pipe thoughtfully. 'I don't know, Carolyn,' he began, slowly. 'If Don Carlos comes tomorrow and I have to tell him that you're staying for an indefinite period, I feel I may find myself on rather uncertain ground.'

'Don't tell him how long I am staying. Say I was in Mexico on holiday, and decided to look you up.'

'And you think he would believe that?'

Carolyn shrugged, but remembering Don Carlos's dark, enigmatic eyes, she doubted it. She had the uncomfortable feeling that he would be perfectly capable of seeing through any artifice she might adopt.

'Well, what are you going to tell him then? Am I

staying? Or are you going to make me go back to that terrible *modern* life in London?' She used the word deliberately, and Professor Madison sighed.

'I don't want to send you back,' he agreed, thoughtfully. 'I was glad to see you were showing a little spunk and initiative by coming here. After all, it is far removed from the life you have always known. But if you stay, you will have to find something useful to do, and something less decorative to wear.' He surveyed her thoroughly. 'That dress would be suitable for the cocktail bar at the Savoy, not the Mexican bush. Haven't you brought any sensible clothes?'

'I don't have any *sensible* clothes,' said Carolyn, a trifle moodily. 'Honestly, what are these men? Sex maniacs, or something?'

The professor laughed at last, and wiped his eyes with the back of his hand. 'All right, Carolyn. All right. You can stay, at least for the time being. But any more exhibitions like this one, and you will have no second chances, is this understood?'

'Yes, Dad.'

'Good. Then I think we can join the others for dinner. We do have a very good cook, and the food is not unacceptable. Plain stuff, mostly, with plenty of soups and stews and so on, but it's usually very tasty, and after a day at the dig, anything tastes good.'

'Some recommendation,' remarked Carolyn, a little dryly, as she followed him to the table.

Set out in the open, a trestle table was set about with wooden seats, and Carolyn was seated with her father on one side of her, and David Laurence on the other. David had not had much chance to speak to her before this, and smiled as she sat down, and said, in an undertone:

'I hear you've had a spot of bother!'

Carolyn stifled her giggle. 'I expect the whole camp has heard,' she murmured. 'But seriously, though, what a fuss! Just over losing my temper!'

'Still, Maddie says you're staying.'

'I'm on probation,' said Carolyn, wrinkling her nose. 'What is this?' as a kind of soup was placed in front of her by a beaming Mexican in a white overall.

'It's delicious,' said David. 'Soup with noodles and vegetables. A Mexican speciality.'

Carolyn tasted it tentatively, and found he was right. It was delicious, and she ate hers with some relish. It seemed hours since lunch at the airport in Veracruz. The dessert was a kind of paste, made of fruit and sugar, and hardened in the sun, called *ate*. It was a little sweet for her liking, but she managed it, and afterwards there was more delicious coffee.

The evening was warm, and sweet-scented, and after the heat of the day was very refreshing. Carolyn lay back in her chair, and smoked a cigarette, listening to the men talking about the day at the dig.

'Where are you digging?' she asked David, as they rose from the table and walked casually across the grass together.

'Over there,' he indicated a mound of earth. 'Beyond that small mound there is lower land, and that's where we're working. Tomorrow you must come and see for yourself. It's quite interesting, even for a novice.' He grinned.

Carolyn smiled at him. He was very easy to get along with, and she supposed he was handsome in a rather boyish way. His hair was brown, flecked with a lighter colour where the sun had bleached it, and he was solidly built although not much taller than herself.

'I doubt whether I'll get that close to the digging,' she remarked, leaning back against the bonnet of one of the Land-Rovers. 'I think my father intends to keep me firmly in the background.'

David chuckled. 'Then I should say he has quite a job in mind,' he murmured. 'Tell me, are you still tied up with that creep Alaistair Kendrew?'

Carolyn drew on her cigarette before replying. 'Alaistair's not a creep,' she protested. 'I admit, he can be rather a bore at times, but I've known him since we were infants, and I guess Merle thinks he's safe.' Merle was her eldest sister.

'And his money's good,' remarked David, dryly.

'Oh, David!'

'Well, it's true. After all, having Lord Berringdon as his uncle is quite a recommendation.'

'Not to me,' said Carolyn, briefly.

'No,' David looked repentant. 'No, you're right. I'm sorry, Carolyn. Come on, I'll take you for a drive to the lake. It's not far from here. We all go there to swim. It's perfectly safe, and you can see Don Carlos's hacienda from the shoreline.' He stubbed out his cigarette. 'It's quite spectacular, and after the horror of the journey here, I guess you could do with some convincing that this place isn't as barbaric as it seems.'

Carolyn hesitated. 'Oh, David, I'd love to, but—but Dad said I hadn't to—well——' Her voice trailed away.

David studied her for a moment. 'What's wrong? What has he said?'

'Nothing really, except that I shouldn't get involved —with anyone.'

'I'm not asking you to get involved,' said David, reasonably. 'Go ask him then; ask him if you can take a ride in the Land-Rover.'

Carolyn sighed. 'You're making it terribly difficult, David.'

David grimaced. 'Why? You know you'll do as you like whatever he says.'

Carolyn frowned. 'No, I shan't! Oh, David. . . .'

'Oh, David, what?' She swung round to face Simon Dean. 'Hello, Carolyn. What has Dave been asking you to do now?'

'Clear off, Simon, there's a good boy,' said David, his light tone belying his annoyance. 'Can't you see, this is a private matter.' He glared at the other man. 'Go write a letter to your wife!'

Simon's face darkened. 'Mind your own business, Dave! Now what can be interesting you both? Are you trying to persuade the professor's fair daughter into getting herself into more bother?'

Carolyn flushed at Simon's sarcasm. 'There's nothing like that, Simon.' She glanced at the broad masculine watch on her wrist. 'Look, it's getting late, and I've had a long day. I think I'll retire and leave you two to your private arguments. Some other time, David.'

David shrugged, and turned away, and Simon said: 'I'll escort you to your tent, Carolyn.'

'That won't be necessary,' replied a familiar voice behind them, and Professor Madison took his daughter's arm. 'Come along, Carolyn.' When they were out of ear-shot, he said: 'You see, already you appear to be causing dissension.'

Carolyn looked exasperated. 'David asked me to drive to the lake with him. He said it's quite spectacular.'

'Yes, Lake Magdalene. Don Carlos's hacienda is at the far side of the lake. It is a beautiful place, but I wouldn't advise you to go swimming at night with any of the men.'

'We weren't going to swim,' exclaimed Carolyn, and then frowned. 'At least, I don't think we were.'

'Dave and Simon often go down to the lake after dinner to bathe. It's the best time of day, and the water is cool and refreshing.'

'I see. Well, David didn't mention that to me.' She sighed. 'I wouldn't have gone, anyway. I'm not that naïve, darling.'

The professor smiled at her. 'No, I don't think you are,' he agreed, nodding. 'Now goodnight. I hope you get a good night's sleep. I hope the crickets don't keep you awake. We're not greatly troubled by them here.'

'Thank you, Dad. Goodnight.' She kissed his cheek and entered her tent, securing the flap after her. Someone had placed a bowl of cold water on the table, and Carolyn washed before undressing. She had brought pyjamas with her, and put them on rather nervously, wondering how much protection was really provided by canvas. Then she switched out the light, and climbed into the camp bed. With its air-mattress it was quite comfortable, but it was all too new and strange for her to be able to sleep.

The darkness outside, after the men retired, was penetrating, and she thought she had never known it could be so black. She could hear the cicadas, as her father had said, and occasionally the strange screaming roar of a mountain lion, somewhere in the hills above the encampment. These sounds were unnerving; the scuffling in the undergrowth around the camp seemed close at hand, and she wondered wildly what she would do if some untamed creature hurtled into her tent.

She sat up abruptly, and reached for her handbag, extracting her cigarettes and lighter. In the small flame of the lighter, the tent seemed filled with shadows, encroaching patches of darkness hiding heaven knew what mysteries, and she hastily put out the light, preferring not to see. Then another sound came to her, a pattering and swell of sound that grew deafening. At first she had no idea what it could be, and she sat still, petrified, until suddenly she relaxed, and almost laughed out loud with relief; it was raining, heavy torrential rain, that beat against the canvas savagely.

She finished her cigarette, and lay down again, listening to the rain. The sound was a familiar one, for all her strange surroundings, and eventually she fell asleep, a faint smile on her lips.

The next morning she was awakened by her father bringing her in a cup of steaming hot tea, which was very welcome. She struggled up, brushing back her hair from her eyes, and screwing up her eyes against the glare of the sun outside.

'Oh lord,' she groaned, tiredly. 'What time is it?'

'Just after six-thirty,' replied her father, smiling. 'I know it's early, but it gets very hot here after midday, and no one works in the heat of the afternoon, so we always start early. You'll probably find you'll take a siesta after lunch and feel completely relaxed and fresh again around four in the afternoon.'

Carolyn grimaced. 'I didn't get to sleep for hours last night. Did you hear that rain?'

The professor laughed. 'No. I usually go out like a light as soon as my head touches the pillow. But I know we have had a heavy downpour by the state of the ground. Fortunately the sun dries everything up very quickly.'

Carolyn nodded in acknowledgement, and sipped the tea. 'What am I to do this morning?' she asked. 'Can I see the dig?'

'I expect so. I'll take you along myself after breakfast. Hurry and dress, and José will have eggs and bacon ready for you——'

'Hold on,' exclaimed Carolyn. 'I don't want eggs and bacon. I usually have a drink of orange juice and some coffee, that's all.'

The professor looked concerned. 'Well, you can't possibly exist on orange juice and coffee until two in the afternoon when we usually have lunch. Okay, if you don't want eggs and bacon, you can have a couple of *tortillas*, have you tried them yet? José does a delicious concoction with fried bananas, I'll have him rustle something like that up for you.'

'No!' Carolyn was horrified. 'Bananas are terribly fattening. I don't want to look like a house-end by the time I leave here!'

'Now, Carolyn, I'm not going to stand here arguing with you.' The professor looked adamant. 'This is Mexico, not London, England, and when in Rome you do as the Romans do, and in this case it means obeying my orders.'

'Oh, Dad! Honestly, coffee will be fine.'

Professor Madison frowned. 'Get dressed. I'll see José and discuss it with him.'

Carolyn slid out of bed, rubbing her eyes. 'All right. All right. But don't be surprised if I only have coffee, anyway.'

After her father had gone, she made a cursory examination of her luggage. Last evening, the cases had been stacked in a corner, and she had only unpacked what she needed. Glancing around she realised that she would not have nearly enough space to unpack all her cases, so she contented herself by hanging a couple of crushable dresses in the polythene stand, and searched through another case for a pair of denim pants, and a pale blue shirt. With her hair tied into a pony tail, she felt more businesslike, and emerged from the tent feeling more ready to face the day.

The men greeted her in a friendly fashion, and she had a few words with Tom Revie before seating herself beside Bill Anderson.

'How did you sleep?' he asked, and she smiled.

'Now I wonder why you should ask that,' she said, lightly. 'Do I look a physical wreck or something? There's a shortage of mirrors around here, so I don't know.'

Bill grinned. 'No, you don't look a physical wreck,' he said. 'You know you look great, as usual.'

'Why, Bill! I do believe that's a compliment,' she teased him, and he flushed, and bent his head to his meal.

The men all seemed to favour the English breakfast, but Carolyn was relieved to find only toast and fresh orange juice beside her plate. The butter was too soft to be really enjoyable, but Bill said that she was lucky to have toast on any terms. *Tortillas* were the Mexican substitute for bread.

After breakfast, Professor Madison came across to Carolyn. 'I'm going up to Don Carlos's hacienda,' he said, solemnly. 'I think it might be a good idea for you to come with me. That way we can get the apology and the explanation all over in one fell swoop.'

Carolyn twisted her fingers together. 'Have you to go? I mean, you're not just going because of me?'

'No. I have to go. Don Carlos has kindly given us the use of a large salon at the hacienda in which we can store all the valuable finds we make. I go up there from time to time to continue with the illustrated inventory I am making. I'm hoping you'll be able to help me with this.'

Carolyn looked interested. 'Oh, really? How good! I shall like having something to do.'

'Good. I'll just have a word with Don and then we'll go.'

The drive to the Alvarez home took them along the borders of the tumbling, restless river which seemed deeper and wider now that they were on a level with it.

'Much of the transport around the state is done by river steamer,' remarked Professor Madison. 'I believe much of the adjoining states is completely unnegotiable except by air and river steamer.'

'Is that a fact?' Carolyn was impressed. 'It seems incredible in this day and age to be so out of touch with civilisation.'

'Parts of Yucatan are still completely unexplored,'

said the professor. 'There may yet be ruins of other Mayan cities lying hidden in the thick jungles.' He sighed. 'If I were a younger man, I should try to get an expedition up to explore more of central America. I find these almost prehistoric tribes, living in circumstances which have not changed for thousands of years, completely fascinating.'

Carolyn shook her head. 'Well, I'm glad you can't go,' she averred, firmly. 'There are head-hunters and cannibals among these tribes. I should be terrified you might not get back alive. I should imagine dozens of explorers have disappeared without trace.'

'I expect many have disappeared, but imagine, Carolyn, what they may have seen before they were—well—possibly killed.'

'I can't see that anything like that could be worth losing your life for,' exclaimed Carolyn.

'Maybe not. You're a woman.' The professor laughed. 'I suppose you are also one of these creatures who abhor bull-fighting.'

'Bull-fighting? I've never really thought about it. I once saw one, in Madrid. It was nauseating.'

'You see,' the professor laughed. 'You haven't the stomach for it. I mention bull-fighting because here it is very popular. In Mexico City there is the largest bull-ring in the world.'

'Of course.' Carolyn nodded. 'The Spanish influence. I didn't think of that.'

'Don Carlos has bred bulls for the bull-ring himself,' went on her father. 'He has also fought the bulls.'

'Don Carlos!'

'Yes. Do you find that surprising?'

Carolyn looked thoughtful, recalling Don Carlos's

tall, lean, hard body. There had been something savage and untamed about him. A kind of leashed violence which was not in keeping with the cold hauteur he had adopted when she had dared to defy him.

'No,' she said, now, shivering a little for no apparent reason. 'I should imagine he could be cruel, and no matter what you say, fighting bulls is a cruel pastime.'

The professor chuckled. 'I would hardly call dicing with death a pastime,' he remarked, dryly. 'However, as we're almost there, we'll leave that discussion for another time.'

The track was winding through semi-cultivated land now, through narrow stretches between the plantations. Then they emerged into the open for a moment before entering tall iron gates and penetrating a belt of tropical trees that was the entrance to the Alvarez hacienda. The scent of jacaranda was almost overpowering, and then Carolyn had her first glimpse of the huge Spanish-designed dwelling. Below the house, lawns and gardens provided a profusion of colour, while the perfumes of the flowers were heady and sensual.

The Land-Rover halted at the entrance to an inner courtyard, and Carolyn slid out, looking up at the colonnaded façade. Tiling of many-coloured mosaics caught the sunlight, and she was impressed. Through the arched entrance to the inner courtyard, she could see a central fountain spilling its sparkling contents into a shallow basin.

Professor Madison came round the Land-Rover to her side. 'Well?' he said, softly. 'What do you think?'

Carolyn shook her head.

'Not exactly what you expected, is it?' he persisted. 'What did you expect anyway? Mud huts?'

Carolyn smiled. 'No, not that. But this is such an isolated spot. One can't believe such a place exists. It's like a small palace.'

'It is beautiful,' agreed her father, preceding her through the archway. 'Come on. It's even better inside.'

Carolyn followed him more slowly, looking about her with interest. The house was built round the central courtyard with balconies to the upper windows. There was a profusion of wrought ironwork and jalousies and shady cloistered arches. Carolyn supposed that was the Moorish influence. She had been in many beautiful houses—stately homes and town dwellings. But never had anywhere completely enthralled her as this place did. There was the bright sunlight, glinting on the fountain, the scent of the flowers, the song of the birds, and the plaintive sound of a Spanish guitar echoing round the secluded courtyard.

She became aware of another presence, and swung round to find her father being greeted by Don Carlos. Today he was dressed in a dark-grey lounge suit, his linen startlingly white against the dark tan of his skin. His thick straight hair had been combed smoothly, but still persisted in lying partly over his forehead. He looked cool and immaculate, and completely sure of himself. In consequence, Carolyn felt a wave of inadequacy sweep over her, and felt a succeeding wave of annoyance follow it. Why should she feel inadequate? She had known plenty of men, and none of them had succeeded in making her feel like this. After all, no matter how important he was in Mexico, he was only a man, after all!

*Only a man!* Carolyn swallowed hard. He was certainly that. She had never known any man emanate such an aura of masculinity, and when his cool grey eyes turned on her she felt young and rather gauche. She knew her father was looking at her expectantly, waiting for her to apologise as she had said she would. But suddenly, she felt rebelliously like forgetting her promise. She remembered how he had crushed the beetle in the shower, and her colour deepened.

With a sigh, she walked across to them. 'Don Carlos, this is my daughter, Carolyn,' her father was saying, and Carolyn halted and allowed her hand to be shaken in a cool, hard grip. She snatched her hand away as soon as she could, and said:

'I—I suppose I should apologise, Don Carlos. I'm afraid I was very rude, the last time we met.'

The man's eyes narrowed a little, and she saw that his lashes were long and thick, veiling his expression. 'I'm sure you were overwrought after your journey,' he answered, smoothly, although there was no warmth in his voice.

Professor Madison looked relieved. 'That is true,' he said, quickly. 'And now, I suppose I should apologise for bringing Carolyn here without asking your permission.'

Don Carlos shrugged his broad shoulders, and Carolyn saw the muscles ripple beneath the expensive material of his suit. She didn't know why but she was aware of everything about this man, and the knowledge was not gratifying.

'I think we will talk much better over coffee,' remarked Don Carlos, suavely. 'Come. We will go to the library.'

Carolyn walked with her father following the man into the building through the wide glass doors. They were now in a mosaic-tiled hall with a wide marble staircase at one side, the balustrade an intricate design of white wrought iron. Don Carlos led the way across the hall, through another archway and into a long narrow room, lined with books, wide french doors opening on to a veranda which overlooked a wide stretch of glistening water.

'Oh, the lake,' exclaimed Carolyn involuntarily.

Don Carlos pressed a button on the desk in the centre of the room, and then turned, looking at Carolyn's animated expression. 'Yes, Lake Magdalene. This is your first sight of the lake, Señorita?'

'Yes.' Carolyn recovered her composure. 'It's very beautiful.'

'And not so *appalling*, Señorita?' he murmured, softly, so that her father who was again lighting his pipe could not hear.

Carolyn stared at him, and then unable to bear the unconcealed contempt in his eyes, turned away. Professor Madison had noticed nothing amiss, and a white-coated servant arrived with a tray of coffee and thin bone china. When the servant withdrew, Don Carlos looked at Carolyn.

'Will you attend to the coffee?' he asked, his tone bland again.

Carolyn wanted to refuse, but instead she nodded, and seated herself beside the tray, asking them their preferences for cream and sugar in a tight little voice. Were it not for her father she would tell *Don Carlos*

*Fernandez Monterra d'Alvarez* exactly what she thought of him!

She was not offered a cigarette, although Don Carlos helped himself to a thin cheroot, and she felt about in her pocket for her own. Finding them, she drew them out and put one between her lips, searching about for her lighter. Don Carlos and her father were discussing the storm the night before and its possible effects on the dig. Carolyn thought she was completely unobserved, but then a gold lighter was flicked and a light applied to the end of her cigarette.

'Thank you,' she said, fuming, and her host merely shrugged and resumed his interrogation of her father.

She looked about her for something to do, avoiding looking in their direction. The veranda outside the french doors was very inviting, and she wondered whether the Alvarez family swam in the lake. There was bound to be a private path giving them access.

And then she found herself looking into a pair of mischievous dark eyes which were peeping round the corner of the door. Carolyn smiled in spite of herself, for she was sure she would never like any member of this family, but the eyes were irresistible. Set in a piquantly attractive face that was much too thin, surrounded by long black hair plaited into two thick braids, the girl was obviously very young.

Surreptitiously Carolyn got to her feet, but the movement attracted Don Carlos's gaze again, and he said: 'Ah, Elena, I thought it was you.' He smiled, and Carolyn stared at him, momentarily hypnotised by the transformation of his lean features. His teeth were white and even, and he was startlingly attractive. Then she forced herself to look away, back at the girl who had now tentatively entered the room, and stood just inside the doorway. She was dressed in a dark-green dress which looked much too old for her, and far too long, and Carolyn thought that in younger, shorter clothes she would be very pretty.

'This is my sister, Elena,' said Don Carlos. 'Elena, this is Professor Madison, and his daughter Señorita Madison.'

'*Hola*,' said Elena, smiling. 'Welcome to the Hacienda Alvarez.'

Carolyn's eyes widened. 'You speak English,' she said, involuntarily.

'All my family have been educated in the United States,' said Don Carlos, smoothly. 'Unfortunately, Elena has been ill and can no longer attend school there. Instead, she has a governess.'

Carolyn looked at Elena with gentle eyes. She did look pale and delicate, but her eyes belied any lack of spirit.

'Where is Señorita Alfonso?' asked Don Carlos, now. 'Surely you should be at lessons.'

Elena laughed irrepressibly. 'I saw the professor and his daughter arrive through my window,' she confessed. 'I wanted to meet Señorita Madison. We so rarely have any *young* visitors to the hacienda, Carlos.'

Don Carlos relaxed a little. 'So now you have met the Señorita, you will return to your lessons, yes? Or Señorita Alfonso will be very cross.'

Elena wrinkled her nose. 'But the señorita cannot be interested in your dull talk, Carlos. Could I not show her the pool, and the lake? And maybe the gardens?'

Carolyn looked at Don Carlos rather sardonically.

Now what would he say?

'I think, Elena, that the señorita will soon be leaving with her father. Besides, I am sure she is not particularly interested in our estate.'

'Oh, but you are wrong, Señor,' returned Carolyn, silkily, enjoying the opportunity of getting her own back. 'I should love to see the pool and the lake and the gardens, and I am sure you and my father are not nearly finished your coffee, yet. I have.'

Don Carlos gave a reluctant nod of his head. 'Very well, if that is what you wish, Señorita.' He looked at Carolyn's father. 'I trust you have no objections, Professor.'

'None at all.' Professor Madison smiled. 'But before Carolyn leaves, perhaps you could tell me whether her presence here in the valley is to be permitted.'

'*Permitted?*' exclaimed Elena. 'Why should it not be permitted, Carlos?'

Don Carlos compressed his lips for a moment. 'Elena, you know nothing about this at all. Please refrain from interrupting.' He looked at the professor thoughtfully. 'I cannot deny that such a permittance is against my better judgement, particularly as the valley is full of men, and I do not really think an archaeological dig is the correct background for a young person like your daughter. After all, she is little older than Elena, and I would not allow Elena to live with a crowd of older men even were I myself present. However, I must accept that the habits and conventions of your society are not as ours, and therefore if you are prepared to take all responsibility for her remaining here, I cannot raise any further objections.'

Carolyn fumed. 'I should point out that I am a

little older than Elena,' she exclaimed, unable to prevent herself.

'Indeed.' He sounded disinterested.

'Indeed, yes,' exploded Carolyn, and then seeing her father's face, she compressed her own lips, angrily.

Elena had watched this exchange with some amusement, and she said; 'Can we go now, Carlos?'

He merely nodded his head, and Carolyn shrugged at her father helplessly and followed Elena from the room. Quite honestly she was beginning to feel exactly like a contemporary of the young Elena's. Whether it was wholly Don Carlos's attitude, or whether the shedding of her sophisticated clothes was responsible, Carolyn didn't know, but what she did know was that Don Carlos's attitude towards her was one of tolerance, mixed with derision, the kind he would reserve for a spoilt and precocious child.

## CHAPTER THREE

OUTSIDE the two girls walked along the veranda until shallow steps led down to the grassy expanse that in turn gave on to a flight of steps leading down to the lakeside. Elena eyed her companion with some admiration, and said:

'You are not afraid of my brother, Señorita?'

Carolyn was annoyed to find her cheeks burned suddenly. 'No. Should I be?'

Elena shrugged. 'I am not afraid of him, but it is usual that he intimidates strangers. He is not an easy person to know.'

Carolyn smiled. She thought Elena's mode of talking was far in advance of her years, and she said: 'How old are you, Elena?'

'I am fourteen years of age,' replied Elena, precisely. 'And you?'

Carolyn shrugged. 'Well, actually, I'm twenty-two, but in your brother's eyes about sixteen, I imagine.' She hunched her shoulders, thrusting her hands into the pockets of her pants. 'Let's forget about that for the time being. Tell me about your life here. Who is this Señorita Alfonso? Your governess?'

'Yes. But she is so *old*!' Elena grimaced. 'She was Carlos's nanny when he was a child, and that is many many years ago.'

Carolyn laughed. 'Oh, not so many, surely.'

'At least thirty-seven,' replied Elena, her eyes wide.

45

'You see, Papa married twice, and my mother was not Carlos's mother; his mother was wholly Spanish. My father met her in Estoril when he was only eighteen. They were very much in love, but unfortunately she died when Carlos was born. Our father married again, I think to give Carlos the security of a complete home. Poor Carmelita, that was Carlos's mother's name. She could not stand the climate here, and in those days the valley was not so prosperous as it is today. Carlos has a helicopter, and he even owns a small aeroplane. It is as necessary here as a motor-car in your country. Much of this area is completely closed to traffic.'

Carolyn nodded. 'I see. And your parents?'

'Oh, both Papa and Mama died in an airliner when it crashed on its way to Mexico City. These mountains are treacherous. No one could survive such a disaster. That was eight years ago now. Since then Carlos and Rosa have taken over the estate. Rosa is my older sister. She is almost as old as Ramon. He is my brother. There are four of us, you see.'

'I see.' Carolyn nodded again, thinking that possibly this was one of the reasons Don Carlos had not wanted her to spend any time with Elena. She was a chatterbox and cared little for conventions.

They reached the foot of the steps and now Carolyn could see a boathouse and a landing stage, and further round, a diving platform. The lake looked cool and inviting, and as the sun rose higher and the day grew hotter she thought how delightful it would be to swim in its depths.

She looked down. It looked deep, even at the rim. 'Do you swim?' she asked Elena.

Elena shook her head. 'Not in the lake. I am not

allowed to do so since my illness. But I swim in the pool. It is always warm. The lake is icy.'

Carolyn smiled. 'It sounds gorgeous! It gets so hot here. Does—does your brother swim in the lake?'

She asked the question compulsively. Despite her averred dislike of Don Carlos Fernandez Monterra d'Alvarez she found she was curious about him. Maybe because in other circumstances she could have found him a challenge. It would be a satisfying feeling to have him attracted to her, desiring her, and being able to subdue that arrogance scornfully.

Elena bent down and trailed her fingers in the water. 'Carlos swims most every day,' she said, in answer to Carolyn's question. 'He prefers the lake to the pool, but it can be dangerous. It's very deep at this side. On the far side—over there,' she pointed, 'there is a sandy shoreline, and I think some of the men from your father's encampment come there to swim.' She straightened. 'It's shallower there. More like the sea.'

'It's very beautiful,' said Carolyn, quietly, looking across the water. Here the humidity was tempered by a breeze from the water, and the brilliance of the sun was reflected in the still depths. Heavy green foliage encroached down to the lakeside, adding its own colour to the scene.

Elena smiled at her. 'Yes, it is. I love it. We were in Acapulco for three weeks but I always am glad when it is time to come home.'

Carolyn walked out along the small jetty. 'Acapulco,' she said. 'I've never been there. Did you see the boys diving from the cliffs?'

'Oh yes. It was very exciting. But there were so many people. I got very tired.'

Carolyn looked up at the hacienda above them. 'You said you were ill; what was wrong?'

'Oh, I had paralysis—I am not sure what you call it. *Infanta*—oh, it's no good. Do you know what I mean?'

'Perhaps you mean polio—poliomyelitis, that is. It can be called infantile paralysis.'

Elena nodded. 'Yes, that was it. I was very ill for over a year. They say I am lucky to be able to walk again. But it has left me very weak, and I soon get tired.'

Carolyn looked compassionately at her. Elena spoke without any sense of self-pity. She seemed to have accepted her condition with complete equanimity. Carolyn admired her courage.

'Come on,' she said now, taking Carolyn's hand. 'If we follow this path we'll come to the steps leading up to the gardens. I'd like you to see the gardens.'

'But—I mean—won't you get too tired?'

Elena shook her head. 'Not if we don't rush. And we do not need to rush, do we?'

Carolyn smiled, and shook her head. 'No. I suppose not.'

The grounds of the hacienda were extensive. There were tennis courts and a swimming pool, flower and vegetable gardens, arbours bright with tropical flowers, bougainvillea spreading its pink and lilac beauty over lacy trellises, and wide stretches of lawn, some adorned with garden furniture and protective striped umbrellas. Carolyn wandered after Elena, completely enchanted by it all, and completely unaware of the passage of time. She only knew that it was getting very hot, and she was beginning to feel uncomfortable out in the sunlight. Just as she thought she would have to tell Elena they would have to return to the library and find her father, they turned a corner of the house and met Don Carlos walking towards them, hands thrust into his pockets, expression thoughtful. Carolyn stiffened, and halted, but Elena merely smiled cheekily, and said:

'I know, Carlos, we have been too long, and I shall take an especially long rest after lunch.'

Don Carlos's expression did not relax. 'I am glad you are aware of your foolishness, Elena. Unfortunately, Señorita Madison, your father could not wait any longer for your return, and in consequence he has returned to the encampment without you.'

Carolyn's eyes widened. 'He's gone! But——'

'Do not alarm yourself, Señorita,' he interrupted her. 'You are welcome to stay here for lunch, and afterwards I will see that you are returned safely to your father.'

Carolyn compressed her lips. She wanted to say that she had no desire to stay at the hacienda for lunch, but Elena's excited voice daunted her. Besides, had she not promised her father to behave?

So all she said was: 'Thank you, Señor.'

He studied her rather hot cheeks intently, and then said: 'I think, Señorita, you have allowed my young sister to keep you out too long in the sun. You are not used to its intensity. Come; Elena, return to your room, and report to Señorita Alfonso. You may say I gave you permission to take Señorita Madison on a conducted tour.'

'Oh, thank you, Carlos. I will,' said Elena, fervently. 'Goodbye for now, Señorita Madison. I will see you at lunch.'

Carolyn smiled. 'All right. And Elena,' as the child turned, 'I think we can dispense with the *señorita*, Carolyn will do.'

'Thank you—Carolyn.' Elena's smile broadened, and she turned and walked away, glancing back occasionally over her shoulder.

Don Carlos took Carolyn's arm rather firmly, and guided her in the opposite direction, through the arched entrance to the courtyard, and in through french doors to a long low lounge. Here the polished floor was strewn with bright rugs, and the furnishings were all in cool blues and greens. In truth, Carolyn was beginning to feel rather light-headed, and when she swayed a little as he released her, he said, harshly:

'Sit down, and if you feel faint put your head down.'

Carolyn stiffened at his cold tone. 'Thank you, but that won't be necessary,' she said, but nevertheless, she did sit down on a low pale green leather armchair, and laid her head back on the cool, smooth upholstery. She would have liked to have closed her eyes against the glare, but with Don Carlos she felt she had to be always on her guard.

He poured out a long cool drink that chinked with ice, and handed it to her. She thanked him and sipped it gratefully. It was lime and lemon laced with some indefinable additive that restored her confidence. Don Carlos poured himself a short drink, and drank it leaning against the cocktail cabinet watching Carolyn with those dark grey eyes. Then he straightened, and lifted a cigarette box off a low table and offered it to her. She took one of the long American cigarettes and allowed him to light it for her before lighting a cheroot for himself.

Carolyn felt uncomfortably aware of his scrutiny, and said: 'The—the grounds are quite beautiful, aren't they?'

He bowed his head in silent acknowledgement of her statement, and Carolyn sought about in her mind for something else to say. She wished he would go and attend to his normal duties and leave her there in peace. But instead he walked across to the french doors and stood with his back to her, looking out on the tiled courtyard. Then he turned, and said:

'I feel the apology you made to me earlier this morning was not sincere. I would like to know why?'

Carolyn was taken aback. 'I—I don't know what you mean.'

'On the contrary, I think you do.' His eyes were narrowed.

Carolyn shrugged, and sipped her lime and lemon. 'As you wish,' she said, carelessly.

Don Carlos walked across the room towards her, and stood looking down at her, putting her at even more of a disadvantage. 'I do not care to be spoken to in that manner, Señorita,' he said, harshly. 'You are a guest in my house, in my valley, but that does not give you the right to act without thought for the feelings of others. I was glad when your father had to return alone to the encampment; it gives me the opportunity to speak with you alone, and to make known my views to you.'

Carolyn felt a little shaky, but she was completely in control of herself as she rose also to face him. 'Please, Señor,' she said, with a touch of insolence. 'Before you start lecturing me I should warn you that I am not one of your peons to be quelled by a hard word from the master! Nor do I like being told what to do and what to say!'

Belatedly, she remembered her promise to her father. But this man was just too much!

Don Carlos's eyes were black and enigmatic. 'It is as I thought,' he ground out, furiously. 'You are a typical product of the permissive society in which you live! You think you can speak to me as you speak to those men back at the encampment, but I can assure you you cannot.'

'Oh no? And how are you going to stop me?' she sneered. 'Do the men in Spanish households beat their women?'

He turned away, and Carolyn thought with a heavy heart that she had really gone too far this time. Why was it that she wanted to shock him like this? What had happened to her normally well-balanced and generous nature? She was acting like a child and speaking like a shrew. If her father ever found out....

'I think we have nothing more to say to one another,' he said, in a chilling tone. 'It is obviously as I thought. Your apology this morning was little more than lip-service, to pacify your father's feelings. However, I still cannot understand why you came here if this is how you feel.'

Carolyn gasped. '*How I feel?* What do you mean, how I feel? You don't know anything about me!'

He drew on his cheroot and turned to face her again, and she thought inconsequently that his hands were long and slim, and how pleasant it would feel to have those hands touch her caressingly.... She brought herself up short. What was she thinking of?

The man was a dictator, impossible to reason with.

'I feel I know quite a lot about you,' he returned. 'For instance, you think that women should be treated as a man's equals; you smoke like a man, a habit I have always personally abhorred in women; you are rude and insolent, and for all you must be eighteen years of age, you act like a spoilt child!'

Carolyn's face burned. 'I am twenty-two years of age,' she exclaimed. 'And women are men's equals, in every way. As for smoking, I am not addicted. I can take it or leave it alone. Anything else?'

'You see,' he lifted his shoulders indolently. 'You must make your point of view clear. These are the actions of a child.'

Before Carolyn could say anything more, he walked to the door. 'I will leave you now. There are matters of the estate to attend to before lunch. One of the servants will tell you when lunch is ready. Excuse me!'

Carolyn inwardly fumed, flinging herself back down on to the chair, drawing hard on her cigarette. She had never encountered anyone even remotely resembling Don Carlos Fernandez Monterra d'Alvarez.

As it happened, lunch was quite a pleasant meal. Elena came to tell her where they were eating, and Don Carlos did not appear during the meal. There was only Elena, and Señorita Alfonso who was in her sixties, and Rosa, the señor's other sister. Rosa was a quiet, attractive girl in her early twenties. Carolyn was surprised she wasn't married, but later over coffee Rosa revealed that the man she had been going to marry had gone on an expedition to the interior of central America, and never returned. Of course, there was still hope, she said, but it was obvious she had given up hope months ago.

After lunch, Elena was sent for her rest, and Carolyn prepared to leave. She wondered who would take her home, and felt her heart drop to her shoes when Don Carlos appeared again.

'Come,' he said. 'I want to see your father, and he will be resting at this time and I will be able to talk with him.'

'All right,' Carolyn said indifferently, and they walked out of the arched courtyard to where a low cream saloon was parked. She had said goodbye to Elena with some regret that she might not see the younger girl again. After all, Elena was a very different proposition from her brother. And that she was lonely there was no doubt.

The car's windows were all open, but Don Carlos mentioned that they were using a saloon instead of a convertible to protect them from the heat of the sun. He also handed her a pair of dark sunglasses which she slid on to her nose with some relief.

Then they set away, the saloon more comfortable than the harder sprung Land-Rover. She thought it was a pity the brilliance of the day could hold so much discomfort, for the scenery was quite spectacular. This afternoon her companion had shed his formal suit and was wearing a cream nylon knitted shirt, and cream close-fitting pants. She couldn't help but be aware of his sexual attraction. There was something wholly sensual about the line of his mouth, belying the cold arrogance he displayed with such vehemence in her presence. She wondered what kind of a man he really was. What he was really like under the façade he always wore in her company. After all, Bill had said he had a fiancée. Surely he was not cold with her; it seemed improbable. After all, he was a Latin, and somewhere he must have all the natural emotions of a man.

She sighed, wondering what sort of a mess she must look by now. She had released her hair from its pony tail, and it was heavy and loose about her shoulders, and probably untidy, she thought. Her shirt was damp and clinging to her back, and she felt unusually tense. She looked across at Don Carlos, and frowned.

'Tell me,' she said. 'Are you going to tell my father about our argument this morning?'

He swung the car round a bend in the road before replying. 'Do you expect me to do so?' he countered.

'Frankly, yes.' Carolyn hunched her shoulders moodily.

'Well, you can relax. I have no intention of causing your father unnecessary anxiety at this time when the state of the dig may be in some difficulties.'

'The dig?' Carolyn exclaimed. 'What has happened?'

'Last night—the storm—much of the excavation was flooded. Naturally this has caused a lot of extra work. This was why your father wished to see me this morning. He required more helpers. I was fortunately able to supply them.'

'I see.' Carolyn sighed again. 'Well, if it's any satisfaction to you, I am sorry for what I said. I'm not usually such a beast. I guess you must just—well—provoke me!' She looked at him again. 'Am I forgiven?'

Don Carlos shrugged his broad shoulders. 'My dear Señorita Madison, you must be absolutely aware that whatever I say you will consider either patronising or insulting.'

Carolyn's eyes narrowed. Was he actually amused now? He looked her way, and she caught the glint of amusement in his eyes. Oh lord, she thought, feeling the heavy pounding of her heart, maybe it's better if he does dislike me. Certainly no man had ever made her feel so nervous all at once.

She looked out of the car windows, trying to calm her emotions. It was ridiculous really. She had known many more strictly handsome men. What was there about him that attracted her? Unless it was that detached hauteur, that made him so different from the men of her experience.

He seemed interested in her expression, for when she glanced his way, his eyes met hers. Floundering, trying to think of something to say, she said the first thing that came into her head:

'Are you always addressed as *Don* Carlos?'

He frowned now. 'Usually. It is a courtesy title, that is all. Why?'

Why? Why had she asked him? She didn't know. Unless of course she accepted that it would be very pleasant to call him just *Carlos*.

'No reason,' she said, now, and wondered how much further it was to the encampment.

'What did you think of Elena?' he asked.

Carolyn cupped her chin with one hand. This was safer ground. 'I liked her,' she said, honestly. 'She told me about her illness. She seems rather a lonely child. Does she have no playmates?'

Don Carlos shrugged. 'There are children from the village, and occasionally we have a visit from our closest neighbours, the Morelos; they have two younger children, a boy of twelve, and a girl of fifteen. They are company for Elena.'

*Morelos.* The name rung a bell in Carolyn's subconscious. Where had she heard that name before? Then she remembered. That was the name of his fiancée, Bill had told her. *Louisa Morelos.* It was an attractive name, and it had stuck in her mind.

'But surely, these visits are not very frequent, and Elena seems to me to need someone now,' she said, and then flushed as Don Carlos's expression darkened.

'I trust you have not been discussing your views with Elena,' he said, coldly.

'Oh no, nothing like that,' exclaimed Carolyn. 'I just felt sorry for her, that's all.' She bit her lip. 'Would you mind if I came over occasionally, to visit her?'

Don Carlos seemed thoughtful. 'We will discuss it some other time,' he temporised. 'See; there is the encampment. We have arrived.'

Carolyn felt he was relieved, and in consequence felt rather disgruntled, herself. It was obvious he had no desire to encourage her visits to the hacienda, and the knowledge annoyed her. After all, Elena was a lonely child, and what harm could she do, just going and talking with her, playing games with her, and generally making her life more enjoyable?

Professor Madison came to greet them, and Carolyn slipped away after the first few sentences. She felt lonely herself suddenly. Her father had not seen fit to confide his troubles to her, and now Don Carlos had again demonstrated his enforced tolerance of her company by revealing his reluctance to have further dealings with her.

She felt dejected. Was she really so objectionable? She had never thought so before, but now she was not so sure.

After a rest on her bed she felt more refreshed, and when she emerged from her tent it was to find that the cream saloon had left. She felt a mixture of relief and regret, and thought that possibly she would now be able to settle down to her stay here.

José, the Mexican cook, surprised her by providing her with a tray of tea, and she thanked him warmly, and sat down in the shade of a large tent which appeared to act as office for the excavation team. It was an untidy conglomeration of papers and charts, and her fingers itched to put things in order. As she was alone, the other members of the party all having returned to the excavation site apparently, she drank her tea and then began sorting through the piles of correspondence. She became so absorbed with her work that she did not realise the time until the sound of men's voices disturbed her. An arm was placed familiarly round her waist, and she sprang back from Simon Dean's embrace.

'Well, well, well!' he said. 'The little office-worker!'

Carolyn thrust him away from her. 'Behave yourself, Simon,' she said, wiping the back of her hand across her damp forehead. 'How are things going? Or daren't I ask?'

'Oh, okay. Who told you we'd had troubles?'

'Don Carlos Fernandez Monterra d'Alvarez,' replied

Carolyn solemnly. 'But really, I wish Dad had told me.'

'Why? There was nothing you could do. As it is, Don Carlos has provided pumping machines, and we've got the whole site drained quite satisfactorily this afternoon. It was pretty bad luck. We've had storms before without any flooding. I think last night's downpour caused a rift in the river bank, and that was why we were so unlucky. However, Alvarez says he will arrange for the river to be repaired, and even raised a little so it could be worse. We've only wasted a day. Without his help we'd have wasted a whole week.' He smiled warmly. 'I must say though it makes a difference to come back here hot and tired and find a beautiful woman waiting for you.'

'I'm not waiting for anyone, Simon, except Dad.' Carolyn smiled. Simon might be a dog in some ways, but he was certainly good for the morale.

Professor Madison looked worn and tired, and retired after dinner that evening. Carolyn had washed in her tent, not risking another encounter in the shower after the day she had had. Then they had eaten some delicious stew with diced chicken and vegetables, heavily spiced, and a pineapple flan. Carolyn was allowed to taste *tequila* for the first time, but she didn't much like it, and when David pointed out that it was made from the cactus plant it made her even less enthusiastic.

She successfully discouraged David's attempts to get her to go out with him, and spent some time in her tent reading before turning out the light. The professor had been too tired to notice her efforts in the 'office' and she had not attempted to tell him. He would find out soon enough; she felt tired, too.

This evening she fell asleep almost immediately, exhaustion catching up with her, but her final thoughts had been of a tall, lean Mexican, with cold grey eyes who refused to see her as anything other than a nuisance.

## CHAPTER FOUR

THE next few days were uneventful. When Professor Madison discovered that Carolyn had tidied up his correspondence and technical papers he asked her if she would like to type out the daily accounts of work undertaken, and Carolyn was pleased to agree. It gave her something to do when the men were at the dig. Although she had been allowed to visit the site with her father he would not allow her to work there judging her too much of a distraction for the younger members of the team. Not that she particularly minded. As far as she could see the slowly appearing bases of what had been imposing temples presented no great excitement, although the relics they had found, knives, pottery, and some wall paintings, fascinated her. These were the things that had been transported to the Alvarez Hacienda, but as one of the team was a photographer they had all been photographed and catalogued along with the other information. Carolyn supposed it would be possible to become enthralled with ancient civilisations, and the huge excavation which stretched some two miles by three along by the river was certainly an important piece of history in its own right. But she was a modern girl, and the actual work involved seemed slow and laborious, and she soon grew bored by watching the men.

She wished Don Carlos had been more willing for

her to visit the hacienda. She could have made a friend of Elena.

One morning, after the men had departed for the dig, she felt restless. There was no typing for her to do, and the limited reading matter she had brought with her had long since been exhausted. Her father had asked her not to leave the camp, but she saw no harm in taking one of the Land-Rovers for a spin. After all, it wasn't as though there were dozens of tracks to lose oneself in, and she had quite a good sense of direction. Without consulting anyone, she collected her swimsuit and a towel, and climbed behind the wheel. She had some vague idea of the direction of the lake, and she hoped that by following the river she would come upon it.

And she did. It was quite a short distance to the near side of the lake, and as she parked the Land-Rover in the shade of a belt of trees she saw the impressive environs of the Alvarez Hacienda sweeping down to the water several hundred yards away.

The shoreline was, as Elena had said, sanded, and she swiftly removed her slacks and shirt, and the scanty underwear she wore, and donned the dark red one-piece suit. Then she trod the gritty sand to the water's edge. It was marvellously cool, and she swiftly moved into the swell, allowing the water to cream over her shoulders, thoroughly soaking her heavy hair. Smiling, feeling a wonderful sense of well-being, she swam lazily out into the sunlight, moving slowly and rhythmically.

It was as she turned on to her back that she saw the small boat drifting towards her. Frowning, she turned and swam back to the shore, wading out of the water, and throwing the huge yellow towel around her shoulders. She thought it was one of the peons from the estate, fishing, but the boat came purposefully towards her, and as it got nearer she saw a man sitting in the stern rowing with lazy strokes. He came close to the shoreline, and shouted:

'Hello! You must be Carolyn Madison. I'm Ramon d'Alvarez.'

'Oh!' Carolyn bit her lip. *Ramon!* Elena's brother.

Now that he was closer she could see that he was about her own age, with thick hair like his brother, a handsome tanned face, but without the cold arrogance Don Carlos exhibited. He beached the boat, and climbed out, dragging it up the beach to prevent it from being cast adrift. Then he came walking towards Carolyn, a lazy smile on his face. Well, she thought, half amused. Were two brothers ever so different?

'So you're Señorita Madison,' he said, admiringly. 'Elena has told me a lot about you. You sounded such a paragon I was eager to meet you for myself. I must admit in some ways she did not exaggerate.'

'Oh no?' Carolyn smiled now, and wrapping the towel about her, she said: 'What are you doing out on the lake?'

'I was fishing,' he replied, glancing back over his shoulder. 'But, as you see, I had no success.'

'How unlucky,' said Carolyn, sardonically, and seated herself on a log nearby, reaching for her cigarettes. Ramon she could understand very well. He was a product of her own generation, and she felt sure his attitudes were not those of his elder brother.

Now he produced a gold cigarette case, and offered it to her with alacrity before taking one himself and then lighting them both.

'You don't object, I gather,' she said, waving the cigarette as she spoke.

'No. Should I?'

She shrugged. 'Your brother does.'

He grinned. 'Oh, Carlos, yes, he would. But then, Carlos is much older than I am. Than *you* are!'

She bent her head. 'And what do you do? Or is that a leading question?'

'Nothing at the moment. I'm at university in California, but on vacation just now.'

'Oh, I see.' Carolyn nodded. 'I thought perhaps you worked for your brother.'

'Carlos? No. At least, not officially. He has a manager to run the estate, and he merely supervises the whole set-up.' He smiled. 'But I like it here, all the same. There are fewer restrictions, although we have fun on the campus. Tell me, Señorita—ah—Carolyn? —did you attend college in England?'

Carolyn shook her head. 'Just a finishing school in Switzerland,' she said, shaking her head. 'And I guess you can call me Carolyn. Señorita Madison sounds so formal.'

'I agree, and I am Ramon, of course.'

'Don't you have one of those long, terribly aristocratic list of names?' asked Carolyn, laughing.

Ramon grinned. 'Oh yes. You mean Ramon Alfredo Mendoza d'Alvarez. This is me! Fortunately in the States I am simply Ramon d'Alvarez, and I can forget the rest.'

Carolyn's laughter pealed again. It was so refreshing to talk to someone young again, someone without ties or inhibitions of any kind. She had almost forgotten such people existed in the days since her arrival.

'Have I interrupted your swim?' he asked, raising a foot to rest it on the log beside her.

Carolyn blew a smoke ring. 'I suppose you have. Do you swim?'

'Most days,' he nodded. 'But I haven't brought my trunks with me, and I don't think you are the kind of girl to agree to anything else.'

His eyes twinkled, and Carolyn could not feel offence at his comments. Instead, she finished her cigarette, and said: 'I think I will go in again. It's getting so hot, and I'll have to return to the camp soon. My father told me not to leave it, but there's very little to do there.'

Ramon nodded, straightening. 'Why don't you come over to the house? I know two people who would be pleased to see you.'

'Your brother practically vetoed that idea,' said Carolyn, dryly. 'At least, he showed no enthusiasm, and quite honestly I have no desire to arouse his anger and by so doing cause trouble for my father and the team.'

Ramon shrugged. 'It is my home too,' he said, with a little of the arrogance Carolyn was used to. 'If I invite you, my brother cannot object. At least no one can say Carlos is impolite to guests in his home.'

Carolyn wrinkled her nose. 'Perhaps not. Nevertheless, I don't think I'll risk it, just the same.'

Ramon looked disturbed, but Carolyn halted any further comment by leaving him, dropping the towel on the log, and entering the water. She saw him put a foot on the end of his cigarette before pushing the boat out into the water and following her. She swam strongly, striking out across the lake towards the middle. It was very cold in the centre, and she wondered with a faint shiver whether it was very deep. It certainly seemed like it.

Ramon had difficulty keeping up with her, but as he came abreast he said: 'Take it easy, Carolyn. This water can be dangerous. I've had cramp here myself.'

'Thanks for the warning.' Carolyn turned on to her back and floated. 'It's marvellously clear, isn't it?' She turned and did a jack-knife under the water, coming up at the other side of the boat.

Ramon smiled, and said admiringly: 'Meet me tomorrow, at the same time, and I'll join you.'

Carolyn could see no harm in that. Surely her father could not object to her being friendly with Don Carlos's brother, and surely Don Carlos himself could read no ulterior motives in her actions either.

'All right,' she said, holding the side of the boat to keep herself afloat. 'What time is it right now?'

'Half after ten. Meet me about nine-thirty tomorrow, right?'

'All right.' Carolyn nodded, and with a wave of her hand she swam back to the shore leaving him to propel himself back across the lake to the Alvarez landing stage.

She was home and her hair dry again before her father returned, and in consequence felt reluctant to reveal her escapade to her father. It was one thing to plead boredom when he found her out in some misdemeanour, but quite another to confess to an unknown offence. For the rest of the day she was in two minds whether or not to tell him, and finally decided against it. After all, what had she done, anyway?

Driven about half a mile and swum in the shallows of a lake that was clear and perfectly safe. What possible objection could he have? She refused to admit to herself that her reasons for finding these excuses for herself were caused by a sense of deceit, and a suspected belief that Professor Madison might have some concrete objections and thus prevent her meeting Ramon the following morning. So she said nothing, and felt terribly guilty about it.

However, the next morning with the sun casting its brilliance over everything, and the prospect of a cooling dip in the lake beckoning her on, she forgot her inhibitions, and left the camp after the men had departed feeling free and exhilarated.

The drive to the lake was accomplished with as little difficulty as before, and as Carolyn had put on her swimsuit before leaving the camp she slid confidently out of the Land-Rover, looking about her expectantly. The beach was deserted and a glance at her watch told her it was already gone half past nine. She hunched her shoulders, but then relaxed as Ramon appeared from beyond close-growing shrubs, wearing only blue-and-white-striped swimming trunks.

'I thought you weren't here,' she said, putting her bag down on the sand and sliding her arms out of the towelling jacket she was wearing over her suit.

He grinned. 'And I thought you weren't coming,' he said, lazily. 'Come and have some coffee.'

Carolyn frowned, but she lifted her bag and beach coat and followed him round the trees until they came upon a more secluded stretch of sand where two airbeds were waiting, plus a small picnic hamper and of all things, a portable record player.

'My, my,' she said, smiling. 'This is nice!'

She seated herself on one of the air-beds, sliding dark glasses on to her nose, and lying back luxuriously. Ramon smiled, and then knelt beside her opening the record player and putting on a record. It was a pulsating beat number that she had heard just before she left England, and she grinned more broadly. 'Home from home,' she said. 'I like that group. I have some of their records back at the camp.'

'Have you?' Ramon was interested. He stretched beside her, and Carolyn deliberately closed her eyes to prevent him from holding her gaze with his. 'You're quite a girl, Carolyn,' he murmured. 'Don't the men back at the camp fight over who is going to sit beside you at meals?'

'Not so's you'd notice,' remarked Carolyn, dryly. 'No, actually my father has made me promise to have no dealings with any of the men at the camp.' She grimaced. 'Actually for camp read Mexico.'

'I don't understand.' Ramon frowned. 'I understand your language quite well, but you have me at a disadvantage at the moment. What do you mean?'

'It means that he doesn't know I've met you, and that he doesn't know I'm here. I guess he would not be entirely enthusiastic about our friendship.'

'Is that so?'

'Yes. Oh, you know how it is! He thinks I can't look after myself.'

'And can you?'

She laughed softly. 'So far. At any rate, I haven't such a low opinion of his sex as he seems to have. Men, I find, generally require some response, and if they don't get it—well—I'm sure you understand.'

He nodded, and with a shrug he lay back beside her. 'You're not at all like the girls here,' he said. 'Spanish women are very proper, if they come from very proper families, that is, and the ones I meet generally do. They would never dream of bathing alone with a man, particularly not wearing such an attractive swimsuit. They would require what we call a *duenna*, a chaperon, if you like.'

'Yes, I have heard,' she said, rolling on to her stomach. 'But however do you manage to court a girl here? I mean, if you're seldom alone, and everything is so—well—proper——'

'Generally marriages are arranged,' said Ramon, sighing. 'Marriage is for convenience, for position, for money, but never for love.'

'How appalling!' Carolyn wrinkled her nose. 'I should hate to have my father pick the man he would like me to marry. The type he would choose would probably bore me stiff.'

Ramon smiled, slanting a gaze at her, his eyes appreciative of the picture she made, her thick honey-coloured hair falling forward round her face, her skin a delicious shade of creamy brown. Thick dark lashes were veiled behind the dark glasses, but he thought she was utterly enchanting.

'They're usually very successful, I have to admit,' he said, thoughtfully, 'although I do agree it's more fun choosing yourself.'

He sat up and produced a flask of coffee from the hamper, and handed her two plastic cups. Then he poured the coffee, and drew out his cigarette case lighting two and handing her one.

It was very pleasant there, and the sun was not yet

uncomfortably hot, sheltered as they were by the trees. Carolyn drank her coffee appreciatively, savouring its aromatic smell.

'And what do you do,' Ramon asked, 'back in England?'

Carolyn shrugged. 'Oh, practically nothing, unfortunately. My father is of the old school of parents who consider their daughters shouldn't have to work if they don't need to. I would have liked to work with children but Dad wouldn't hear of it, and so...' Her voice trailed away.

Ramon studied his coffee. 'And you're not engaged—or married?'

'No.' Carolyn smiled. 'I suppose you think at twenty-two I'm over the hill.'

'Don't be silly. Of course not. I've no particular desire to be married myself.'

'Yes, but men are different.'

'That annoys you?'

'A little.'

'Why?'

'Well, it shouldn't matter, should it? I mean, where is the difference? I'm convinced the idea of women being wives and mothers and nothing else is a hangover from some era where only the attractive females got married and if you weren't married you were considered a hag.'

'And don't you think that only the attractive women get married today?' Ramon was fascinated by the ever-changing expressions flitting across her mobile face.

'Of course not. Heavens, look around you! Half the most sought-after women in the world would have been considered ugly fifty years ago. Today men have realised that a woman's mind can be equally as fascinating as her body.'

'I'd go along with that,' said Ramon, grinning, and Carolyn pushed him back on the air-bed playfully and rose to her feet.

'I'm going for a swim,' she said, and ran swiftly into the cold waters of the lake.

Ramon followed her, and they played in the water for some time, splashing each other, and racing towards the side of the lake where it curved round to their left. Then they came back up the beach, shaking the water from their bodies like puppies. Carolyn wrung out her hair, and lay back on the air-bed.

'I'll have to go soon,' she said, regretfully, sliding her glasses back on to her nose.

'Not yet,' said Ramon, lying on his stomach beside her, and looking down into her face. 'Will you come again tomorrow?'

'I don't know,' she said, closing her eyes again.

'Please,' he said, softly and insistently.

Carolyn deemed it was time to make a move to go. She sat up and pulled on her beach coat. Then she gathered her things together, and rose to her feet.

'Well,' she said, looking down at him. 'I may just do that. Come tomorrow, I mean.'

'I'll be here,' he said, softly, and Carolyn smiled, and nodded, and turning walked back to the Land-Rover.

For a week she met Ramon at the lake every day. If her father and the other men wondered how she filled her time, they didn't worry, and as Don Carlos came to the site only rarely, and then when Carolyn was invariably resting after lunch, she did not have to face any questions from him.

There had been some heavy downpours during the evenings, and the workers at the dig had been kept busy keeping the site clear. The river was slowly being dammed and when this was done the danger would be over.

Carolyn managed to keep up to date with the typing, and occasionally in the cool of the evening she played cards with her father, Donald Graham, and Tom Revie. She learned bridge, and even began to enjoy it. Occasionally she played her record player but mostly she took the records to the lake with her and played them there on Ramon's record player. Occasionally she felt twinges of conscience that she should deceive her father in this way, but he seemed so absorbed in his work that he did not pay a great deal of attention to Carolyn whenever she attempted to bring the conversation round to her affairs.

Two days later, the calm was shattered. Carolyn, unaware of anything amiss, drove as usual to meet Ramon. It was another marvellous morning and she sang softly to herself as she parked the Land-Rover beneath the trees. Ramon came to meet her, dressed in cream shorts and a blue sweater. He looked at her with something more than mere friendliness in his eyes, and Carolyn wondered whether she wanted him to feel this way about her. He was very nice, and fun to be with, but somehow she didn't want to spoil the kind of gentle companionship they had shared. Although in some ways he was brash and sophisticated, in others he was absurdly sensitive, and she didn't want to have to hurt his feelings, Consequently, she had determinedly kept him from becoming emotionally involved with her. But daily it was growing more difficult, and she thought that possibly she might have to stop meeting him every day.

But just now, she thrust these thoughts away, and walked to meet him, smiling. 'You're early,' she said. 'It's not nine-thirty yet. I left the camp sooner than I usually do.'

Ramon looked down at her intently. 'Every day I am earlier,' he murmured, caressingly. 'Our time is too swiftly over.'

Carolyn moved away from his intensity. 'Don't let's be serious, Ramon,' she said, lightly. 'Have you brought the boat with the outboard motor? And the water-skis, like you said?'

Ramon compressed his lips moodily. 'Yes, I've brought them. But can't we have a cigarette before we start?'

Carolyn looked back at him, saw the pleading expression on his face and relented. 'All right,' she said, nodding.

In their secluded corner of the beach, Carolyn accepted a cigarette and drew on it luxuriously. If she did stop meeting Ramon she would miss these beautiful mornings here.

Ramon seated himself beside her, and Carolyn suddenly felt overwhelmingly conscious of their isolation. She was wearing only a black bikini, a black-and-white-striped towelling jacket hiding her smoothly tanned limbs.

'What's the matter?' he asked, with acute perception. 'You seem different, somehow. Have I offended you in some way?'

Carolyn smiled wryly. 'No, of course not. Tell me,

Ramon, do you tell your brother that you're meeting me?'

Ramon shrugged. 'Why should I? It's nothing to do with him.'

'Isn't it? I thought everything in this valley was to do with him.'

Ramon looked annoyed. 'I handle my own life.'

Carolyn compressed her lips, and lifted the heavy swathe of her hair off her neck for a moment allowing the cooling breeze to reach the skin. Ramon leaned forward and she felt the cool touch of his mouth against the nape of her neck.

'How *delightful*!' The sardonically cold voice almost petrified Carolyn with shock, and her cheeks burned annoyingly as she looked up to find Don Carlos standing a few feet away, looking dark and angry, and disturbingly attractive. Dressed in dark blue close-fitting trousers and a loose cream sweater he looked cool and arrogant, and both Ramon and Carolyn scrambled to their feet like two children caught out in some mischief.

'What are you doing here, Carlos?' asked Ramon, angrily. 'Have you followed me?'

'What? And demean myself by behaving like an amateur private eye!' Carlos shook his head. 'I found out about your liaison quite innocently. Pedro Sanchez asked me how long Anna was staying because he had seen you with her down at the lake for the last week or so.' His lip twisted. 'I prevaricated; I had no intention of revealing that my own brother was meeting another woman.'

Carolyn stared at Ramon, seeing the dull flush creeping up his cheeks.

'So, Ramon, you will return to the house. I will wish to speak with you later in the day.'

Carolyn's eyes widened. Surely Ramon would not take that.

But Ramon said: 'Look, Carlos, I'm no teenager to be bossed about. I'm twenty-three.'

'I know it. I also know that you are under my jurisdiction until you are twenty-five by the terms of our father's will!' He ground out the words.

Ramon bent his head. 'Hell, Carlos——' He stopped and looked at Carolyn reluctantly, but she turned away, feeling furiously angry and impotent all at the same time. Without another word, he turned and walked away to where his car was parked.

After he had gone Carolyn glanced round surreptitiously, hoping against hope that Don Carlos would have gone also. Of course he had not.

'Well?' she said, putting her hands on her hips. 'What did I do wrong now?'

Don Carlos lit a cheroot with slow, deliberate movements. Then he shrugged his broad shoulders. 'Don't you know?'

'If I did I wouldn't be asking!' she retorted, insolently, and succeeded in straightening his mouth and darkening his eyes.

'Then I'll tell you. Ramon is an impressionable young man, unused to being—how shall I put it?—on such *friendly* terms with a woman, not of his own kind.'

'Kind? What do you mean, *kind*? Maybe you mean his own class?'

Don Carlos ignored her outburst, and continued: 'Maybe in your country men who are legally bound to one woman can have—well—a relationship with another woman. Here things are a little different.'

Carolyn grimaced. 'I don't like your descriptions,' she exclaimed. 'Ramon and I have not had a *relationship*, certainly not of the kind you insinuate. Neither do I understand what you mean when you say legally bound; is Ramon married or something?'

'Or something. He is betrothed to Anna Costilho, the daughter of a great friend of mine, Manuel Costilho.'

'Engaged! Oh, I see.' Carolyn kicked her toes in the sand. 'It may come as a shock to you to learn that your *little* brother didn't reveal his engagement to me!'

Don Carlos looked sceptical. 'You expect me to believe that?'

Carolyn stared at him. 'Just what do you mean by that remark?' His attitude as always brought out the worst in her.

Don Carlos merely drew on his cheroot and turned away. It was obvious he had no intention of arguing with her.

Carolyn was incensed. How dare he come here and treat her like some—like some cheap harlot, his brother had picked up in a downtown tavern?

Carolyn ran to catch him up, keeping pace with him with difficulty. 'I don't know what kind of women you are used to dealing with,' she stormed, 'but if they fit the categories you've been describing to me, then I'd say it's me, and not your sainted brother, who ought to be more selective when picking friends!'

He halted momentarily, and she thought she had really roused him, and then he smiled, rather sardonically, and said: 'Save your explanations, Señorita. I can see that you are distraught, and perhaps a little hurt. This is natural, of course, Ramon is an attractive young man, but I am sure you will find your compatriots back at the camp more than willing to assuage your shaken pride!'

Carolyn's hand darted up and slapped him hard across his cheek. He stared at her almost in disbelief, and then, before he could retaliate, she ran the remaining few yards to the Land-Rover and sliding in swiftly thrust it into gear, the wheels churning up the earth beneath their grip.

She felt a vague feeling of fear, looking back through her rear-view mirror, to see him standing watching her, one hand raised to the cheek she had slapped. He looked absolutely furious, and her heart thumped wildly when the Land-Rover groaned momentarily in protest, as the tyres squealed on the track. She thought she was going to stall it, but it picked up again, and then she was out of sight.

She drove back to the camp at top speed, and did not feel safe even when the walls of her tent closed securely around her.

## CHAPTER FIVE

For the next few days Carolyn lived in fear of Don Carlos coming to the site and ordering the whole team off his land. If that happened she knew she would feel really bad. After all, no matter what explanations she might offer, her father would be far more likely to accept Don Carlos's indignation than her own.

But nothing happened, and she felt an unreasonable dejected feeling taking hold of her. She thought it was entirely to do with the ending of her visits to the lake, but she knew that was not all of it. She didn't like being accused of something for which she was innocent. Surely Ramon must have told his brother that he had not revealed his engagement to her.

Then, one morning when she was sitting in the tent with all the office equipment, a low-slung red convertible came smoothly across the grassy stretch to park not far from where she was working. Carolyn glanced round, and then pressed a hand to her stomach. Don Carlos was sliding out of the driving-seat, but he was not alone. With him was a small, delicately proportioned Spanish girl, with heavy black hair coiled up the nape of her neck, and when Don Carlos assisted her from the car Carolyn saw she was wearing a brilliantly coloured green two-piece with a wide flared skirt and a close-fitting bodice that accentuated the small waist and pointed breasts. Beside her, Carolyn felt like an unsophisticated, inelegant teenager, unaware that in the close-fitting blue pants and open-necked white shirt she was wearing, her honey-coloured hair straight and thick about her shoulders, she looked tall, a little voluptuous and the picture of health.

Then Carolyn saw that Elena was bouncing excitedly in the back of the car, waiting for Carlos to hold forward his seat so that she could get out. When he did so, she jumped out and dashed over to Carolyn saying:

'Carolyn, you've never been to see me!' reproachfully.

Carolyn glanced at Don Carlos, saw the dark eyes veiled by his thick lashes and returned her gaze to Elena.

'I'm sorry, honey,' she said, lightly. 'As you can see I've been busy.'

She looked across at the girl with Elena's brother. She had guessed that this must be Louisa Morelos, his fiancée. Don Carlos said something to Louisa, and she smiled prettily up at him and sliding her arm possessively through his they walked across to where Carolyn and Elena waited.

'Louisa, I'd like you to meet Señorita Madison, the good professor's daughter,' said Don Carlos, smoothly. 'Señorita Madison, this is my fiancée, Louisa Morelos.'

'How do you do?' Carolyn thrust her hands into the pockets of her pants, avoiding any kind of contact with the other woman. There was something faintly repulsive to Carolyn about the way Louisa held on to Don Carlos so securely. Almost as though she was afraid of losing him, thought Carolyn, cynically.

'How do you do, Señorita Madison.' Louisa was looking at Carolyn speculatively. 'I hear you are living here, at the camp.' She brushed her skirt fastidiously. 'Don't you find it all rather—well—primitive?'

Carolyn hid a smile. 'Frankly, yes,' she said, her eyes challenging those of Don Carlos for a moment. Then she looked back at Louisa. 'But we enjoy it, the mad British!' She laughed.

Don Carlos tightened his lips. 'Come Louisa,' he said. 'I wish to speak with Professor Madison.'

'Can I stay with Carolyn?' asked Elena, frowning. 'I don't want to go with you.'

Don Carlos frowned himself. 'It is obvious that Señorita Madison is busy,' he said, coolly. 'We would only be disturbing her.'

'On the contrary,' retorted Carolyn. 'Elena won't disturb me.'

Her eyes were challenging his again. She felt a strange feeling in the pit of her stomach remembering their last encounter. Was he remembering it, too? Had anyone ever slapped his face before? She doubted it. But was that all there was to it? His eyes were dark, compelling, and she shivered in spite of the heat of the day. She had the feeling that Don Carlos Fernandez Monterra d'Alvarez never forgot an insult. She suspected he could be very cruel.

He turned away. 'Very well,' he said. 'We will not be long. Your father is at the site, I presume, Señorita?'

Carolyn shrugged. 'Yes.'

'Good. Come, Louisa.'

Louisa ran the end of her tongue over her red lips.

'Please, Carlos *querido*, I will stay with Señorita Madison, also. After all, it looks rather muddy over there, and my shoes...' Her voice trailed away, while all eyes appraised the slender strapped sandals on her dainty feet.

'If you insist.' Carlos's voice was cool and impersonal, and with scarcely a backward glance he strode away.

Carolyn studied Louisa for a moment, and then she said, indifferently: 'Would you like some coffee, Señorita Morelos?'

Louisa's eyes were less openly friendly now. 'Yes, thank you. Elena, shall we sit in the shade of the tent. It is not good for you to be out too long in the sun.'

Carolyn thought cynically that what Louisa really meant was that the sun was not good for *her* complexion. She had the magnolia white skin sometimes found on Spanish women, and Carolyn felt sure she would never dream of sunbathing and allowing that immaculate complexion to get burned. She rubbed her nose a trifle ruefully as she thought of her own brown skin and then smiled to herself. With her hair a white skin would look unnatural, and besides, who wanted to have to guard their skin twenty-four hours a day?

Elena ignored Louisa however and skipped after Carolyn as she walked across to the cookhouse. José was there, idly reading a newspaper, but he jumped to his feet when he saw Carolyn. He had a soft spot for her, and in the last few weeks he had come to know her quite well during the time when they were the only occupants of the encampment.

The tray of coffee was soon ready and Carolyn

wondered what the polished Louisa Morelos would think of the sturdy earthenware crockery and thick beakers. Whether Louisa had any comment or not she did not voice it but instead began asking Carolyn a lot of personal questions which Carolyn found rather annoying. In a short time Louisa knew most of the general details about her, and Elena was beginning to move about restlessly, poking into cupboards, opening filing cabinets, and interfering with the typewriter.

After preventing her from muddling up a pile of photographs Carolyn said: 'Come on, Elena. I'll take you on a sightseeing tour. I'm sure Señorita Morelos will wish to stay here. The site is muddy in places and the sun is *very* hot!'

Louisa looked annoyed. 'Where are you taking Elena?' she asked, shortly. 'Naturally as Carlos is not here, I am responsible for her.'

Carolyn wrinkled her nose. 'You don't think I am capable of taking care of a fourteen-year-old, is that it?'

Louisa looked patient. 'That is not it at all, Señorita Madison. I merely don't think you should take Elena out in the hot sun.'

Carolyn shrugged. 'How about you, Elena?'

Elena grinned. 'I'm fine. I spend hours out in the mornings. It's not so hot, Louisa. You stay here and rest. We won't be long.' She looked up at Carolyn. 'Carolyn likes the same things I do, and we spent hours together one morning up at the hacienda.'

'Señorita Madison is possibly more your age group, I would agree,' remarked Louisa, cattily. 'However, I do not think your brother would approve.'

'Oh, lord!' Carolyn raised her eyes heavenward.

'We'll see you later, Señorita.'

Leaving Louisa still protesting they walked across the encampment together.

'Isn't she terrible!' exclaimed Elena. 'She doesn't want anyone to enjoy themselves but her.' She squeezed Carolyn's hand. 'Where are we going?'

'Well, I thought you might like to see the site, where the men are working,' said Carolyn, smiling. 'We can go this way. It takes a little longer but at least we won't encounter your brother on our way.'

Elena giggled. 'I love the way you talk to Carlos. No one has ever spoken to him like that before. Not even Louisa. She always simpers and pleads, ever so silkily, and he still goes his own way. She can't see it, of course. He let's her think she's making all the decisions.'

'Oh, Elena!' Carolyn laughed merrily, and looked down gently at her companion.

They came upon the site from the river side, and Carolyn knew her father was working at the far side, nearest the camp. Here there was less actual excavation done, and David, who was a geologist, was seated on a folding canvas stool, smoking and studying some data in his hand. He looked up in surprise when he saw Carolyn, and then grinned when he saw Elena.

'Well, hi,' he said, putting down his papers and standing up. He pushed the canvas hat he was wearing back to the back of his head, and came over to them. 'What gives?'

Carolyn lifted her shoulders casually. 'Elena came with Don Carlos, and his fiancée, and she didn't want to hang around the camp while Don Carlos was seeing Father so I told her to come with me.'

'I see. Well, Elena, what do you think of it?'

Elena looked at the half-overgrown expanse of country that was gradually being brought under control by the Spanish-Indian labourers lent to the team by Don Carlos. Here the profusion of greenery was gradually being pushed back to reveal uneven mounds of earth which Professor Madison had told Carolyn hid the remains of the city they had discovered. It would take many months yet before the whole site was laid bare and Carolyn thought the amount of work involved in an adventure of this kind was colossal.

'I don't think it looks very exciting,' said Elena, screwing up her nose. 'But I think some of the things Carlos has up at the house are pretty.'

David nodded. 'Oh yes, the relics. Yes, the pottery looks quite beautiful when it is cleaned. And it is exciting, Elena, if you try to imagine that the people who lived in this city, who worshipped in these temples, lived so many hundreds of years ago. Can you imagine who may have stood on the same spot that you are standing on now? That maybe a tribal battle was fought where your hacienda stands.'

Elena's face lit up. 'Oh yes,' she exclaimed. 'That does sound exciting. Were there really houses here, long ago?'

David smiled at Carolyn. 'Yes. Look, see this stonework here. We believe this was once a religious altar. Can you see the carving? It's quite intricate, isn't it? And the tools they used were not electric or motor driven. This was all done by hand. Can you imagine that?'

David had caught Elena's interest, and Carolyn

looked on smiling. It was doing the child good, being with other people, not cooped up in the hacienda grounds, no matter how grand and extensive they might be.

They were all on their haunches examining David's charts when they heard voices coming in their direction and Elena looked up and said:

'Oh, look! It's your father and my brother, Carolyn.'

Carolyn glanced wryly at David, and they both got to their feet, David helping Carolyn with a casual hand. Carolyn deliberately held his hand longer than was necessary and he glanced at her strangely, and then looked thoughtfully at the arrogant lord of Zaracus.

Don Carlos halted beside them, frowning. 'Elena! What are you doing here? I left you back at the camp—with Louisa!'

Elena turned up the corners of her mouth. 'Louisa is still at the camp,' she said. 'But we were bored, weren't we, Carolyn?'

Carolyn, conscious of her father's eyes on her, said: 'Elena naturally wanted to see the site. So I brought her. She's quite safe with me, Don Carlos!'

He did not reply but merely said, to the professor: 'I think we have covered everything, *amigo*. Come, Elena!' His eyes flickered from David to Carolyn and then back to David again, and Carolyn could almost read his thoughts. She thrust her hands back into the pockets of her pants, tossed her head negligently, and walked away herself back towards the encampment.

As she neared the circle of tents, Elena went running

past her, and Carolyn glanced round to find Don Carlos close behind her. She quickened her step but a moment later she felt his hard fingers close round the soft flesh of her upper arm in an almost vice-like grip, hurting her by its intensity.

'A moment, Señorita,' he said, coldly, halting her progress.

Carolyn tried to free herself, but it was to no avail. He would not let her go.

'I'll scream!' she threatened, pulling away from him.

'Oh yes?' His tone was unpleasant. 'And who will come running? The good professor, or maybe that young man, Laurence? Was that his name?'

'What do you want? I should have thought we had nothing to say to one another,' she protested.

'On the contrary, I have something to say to you.'

Carolyn felt a tingle up her spine. He was so close she could smell the faint male odour about him, a mingling of shaving lotion and tobacco and the heat of his body. She could see the thick mat of hairs just appearing above the open neck of his shirt, and the brown column of his throat.

'Are you wanting an apology?' she asked, trying to retain her composure, her tone sneering.

'I wish to say that you will never do such a thing as strike me again,' he muttered, in a low incensed tone. 'Or you may find the consequences quite frightening!'

'Then don't make me!' she said, fighting off a desire to touch him. She wondered what he would do if she allowed her body to rest against him, and slid her bare arms round his neck. The thought was intoxicating, there in the warmth and heat of a Mexican morning, and her eyes grew warm and hazy.

As though sensing the change in her attitude his eyes dropped to her mouth, resting there for a brief yet electric moment of time, and then he let her go and without another word left her.

Carolyn stood there after he had gone, breathing hard. Her heart was pounding in her chest, and she felt almost giddy with relief, and yet she felt breathless, her whole body warm with perspiration. She leant weakly against a tree-trunk, listening for the sound of the car which would indicate the departure of Carlos, Louisa, and Elena, and a few minutes later she heard just that sound. Sighing, she straightened, and walked back to the encampment.

That evening Professor Madison came to her tent before dinner. Carolyn was applying a cleansing cream to her face, and said: 'Who is it?' almost nervously, when he tapped on the canvas of her entrance.

'Your father,' came the reply, and she relaxed.

'Oh! Come in, Dad.'

Professor Madison entered the tent, dropping the flap back into place, then he drew out his pipe and stood looking at her thoughtfully. Carolyn looked up. 'Is something wrong?'

He shook his head. 'Not exactly.' He frowned. 'This is—rather difficult for me, Carolyn. Tell me, what did Don Carlos say to you this morning?'

Carolyn flushed. 'What about?' she asked guardedly.

'Carolyn, please. Don't prevaricate. I saw him—well —stop you. On your way back to the camp this morning.'

'Oh, I see.' Carolyn bent her head.

'You seemed to be trying to get away. Carolyn, tell me, please. What is going on? If there is anything you can't handle——'

'Oh, *Dad*!' She screwed the lid back on the jar of cream. 'It's nothing like that.'

'Then what is it? To my knowledge you have only met him twice before. The day you arrived, and the day we went up to the hacienda. Why should he behave so much out of character. What did you say to him that day at the hacienda?'

What hadn't she said, she thought gloomily? 'Look, love,' she said, allowing her tongue to play round her lips. 'This morning Don Carlos was angry with me. That is all.'

'But why was he angry?' The professor sighed. 'What have you done now?'

Carolyn grimaced. 'Nothing much. Please, Dad, don't catechise me. Don Carlos and I understand one another very well.'

Her father shook his head. 'So you won't tell me. Carolyn, I thought we were real friends, as well as father and daughter.'

'We are. But this is something you just wouldn't understand. Carlos d'Alvarez is a product of arrogance and omnipotence. He doesn't take kindly to opposition, particularly from the opposite sex. He likes his women meek and mild. That's all. That's why he was angry, I guess.'

'And it had nothing to do with Ramon d'Alvarez?'

'Ramon?' Carolyn's colour deepened. 'What do you know about Ramon?'

'I know you were meeting him every morning for

about ten days down at Lake Magdalene.' Carolyn gasped. 'Is there anything else I should know?'

'You *knew*?'

'Of course I knew. You didn't imagine I never came back to the camp during your absences, did you? José knew where you had gone.'

'Oh lord.' Carolyn rested her chin on her hands. 'So I suppose you think I'm deceitful, too. I would have told you, but I thought you'd object.'

Professor Madison smiled wryly. 'Why should I object? Ramon d'Alvarez is not a wolf in sheep's clothing. I have always thought he was a nice, reliable boy.'

Carolyn wrinkled her nose. 'Did you also know that that nice, reliable boy was engaged to be married?'

'Heavens, no! Is he?'

'Yes. To a girl called Anna Costilho. Have you heard of her?'

'Vaguely. There's a man—Manuel Costilho——'

'Her father,' said Carolyn, heavily. 'Well, Ramon certainly did not tell me, but you try convincing Don Carlos of that. I think he thinks I'm a cross between Jezebel and Bathsheba. At any rate, he hasn't a very high opinion of my morals. Also, he probably doesn't agree with mixed bathing.'

Professor Madison laughed. 'Oh, Carolyn,' he said, shaking his head again. 'You're incorrigible! But at least you've lifted a weight from my mind. I thought Don Carlos was molesting you.'

'Molesting me?' Now Carolyn laughed. 'Darling, there's not much hope of that. Beside Louisa Morelos I feel like an overgrown schoolgirl.'

Now the professor was contradictory. 'Louisa Morelos

may be small, and beautifully proportioned, but she has not got your height and carriage, Carolyn. Besides, I know which I should prefer, and it wouldn't be that milk and water apology for a woman.'

'Oh, Dad!' Carolyn smiled. 'You're very good for my morale.'

But later that night, as she lay in her bed, she wondered what Louisa was really like. She didn't seem very animated for one so young, and seemed to rely on a kind of clinging appeal to attract Don Carlos. But after all, that was exactly the kind of woman he needed; one to agree to his every wish and to merely act as hostess in his home. To bear his children, without a great deal of passion being involved, and to share his life. Carolyn rolled on to her stomach. What a ghastly prospect, she thought, burying her face in the pillow. To marry a man without being in love with him. Maybe Louisa did love Carlos, but Carolyn couldn't imagine her being particularly demonstrative, and she thought that the Spanish girl was hardly likely to lose her self control whatever her circumstances. Her mind turned to Carlos d'Alvarez. He at least exhibited emotions, strong emotions, even if they were only emotions of anger towards her. She thought he might find marriage with Louisa less than satisfying physically. She sighed. What thoughts to be having! Anyone would think she was interested which was ludicrous!

A few days later the red convertible again came to the encampment. Carolyn stiffened but it was Rosa d'Alvarez who slid from behind the wheel.

'Hello, Señorita Madison,' she said, warmly. 'I am so

glad to see you.'

'Me!' exclaimed Carolyn, ungrammatically. 'Why me?'

'Because I have a favour to ask you.' said Rosa, compressing her lips and glancing round. 'Is there somewhere where we can talk?'

Carolyn hesitated only momentarily. 'Yes. My tent. Come on, it's over here.'

Once in the tent Rosa seated herself on the only chair and looked thoughtfully at Carolyn.

'Señorita,' she began.

'Make it Carolyn,' said Carolyn, at once.

'All right. Thank you, Carolyn.' Rosa twisted her gloves. 'As you may know, my sister Elena is taught and cared for by a Señorita Alfonso. Señorita Alfonso was mine and Ramon's nanny, and Carlos's too, for that matter. And she is old, and a little tired.'

Carolyn nodded. 'Go on.'

'Well, Señorita Alfonso was caught out in one of these frequent storms we have been having, and was soaked to the skin. She has, in consequence, caught a severe chill, and our doctor has confined her to her bed for at least a fortnight. I am at my wits' end to know how to deal with Elena. She is quite a handful, and as I have the running of the house to attend to I do not have a lot of time to spend with her. Carlos is away at the moment, and there is no one but Ramon and me at the hacienda, apart from the servants, of course.'

'Of course.'

Carolyn turned away. 'I was hoping I might persuade you to come to the hacienda, to stay with us for a while, and in return to spend some time with Elena.'

Carolyn swung back. 'Me! To stay at the hacienda? Oh, no. I don't think so—Señorita——'

'Rosa, just Rosa.'

'Very well, then, Rosa. You obviously don't realise that I and your brother simply do not get on! If he were to return and find me there...' Carolyn shook her head.

'Oh, Carolyn, *please*. Forget about Carlos. Good heavens, if he returns there is no necessity for you to meet. The house is large. You could eat in the nursery wing with Elena. It was Elena's idea that you should be requested to do this for us. But I must admit I thought it was a very good idea.'

Carolyn sighed. 'Elena is a lonely child. I have thought so before. When I mentioned this to Don Carlos he was not prepared to encourage me to visit the hacienda. I think actually he may consider me a bad influence on Elena.'

'Oh! What nonsense!' Rosa was impatient. 'Well, I am asking you, and I will take the responsibility. *Please!* At least consider it. I'm sure your father will not disapprove.'

Carolyn shrugged her shoulders. 'But to go and stay at the hacienda.... Couldn't I just drive up in the mornings and back at night?'

'You could. But that would not be a satisfactory arrangement. Elena needs someone there all the time, someone she can rely on. Señorita Alfonso slept in the adjoining room to Elena's. Now she has been moved. You could have that room. Oh, won't you come, Carolyn? There's the pool, and the lake! You might even enjoy it.'

Carolyn hesitated. There was also Ramon.

'I'd like to help you, Rosa,' she said, awkwardly, thrusting her hands into her pockets. 'But I've got used to being here, at the encampment. I quite like it, in some ways. The washing facilities are pretty primitive but otherwise it's very relaxing. I wear nothing but pants and shirts all day long, and I've forgotten what it's like to dress properly for a meal.'

Rosa smiled. 'These are only excuses, Carolyn. You know very well you would like to wear dresses again, if only for a change.'

Carolyn hunched her shoulders. 'Well, maybe I would. But not at the hacienda.'

Rosa got to her feet. 'Think about Elena,' she said, softly. 'I know it's a kind of blackmail but she needs you, she really does.'

Carolyn lit a cigarette when Rosa refused, before replying. 'And if I did come; I don't want you to suggest paying me for my services. I mean, I'd be a completely free agent. If I wanted to leave, that would be okay?'

Rosa shrugged. 'If that's what you want.'

Carolyn looked thoughtful. 'How long is your brother away?'

'Carlos? Well, he's gone to the Morelos' home, where his fiancée lives. Her brother is having a twenty-first birthday party. We were all invited, but Elena didn't want to go, and I couldn't leave her alone. As for Ramon, he seems disinterested in anything at the moment.'

'Does he?' Carolyn nodded slowly. 'And so, how long is he away?'

'Oh, a week at least. Señorita Alfonso may be on the mend before he returns.'

Carolyn smiled. 'You're determined to have me go with you.'

'I know. I shall enjoy your company, too.'

'Well, all right, so long as my father approves.'

Rosa squeezed her hand. 'Oh, thank you, thank you, Carolyn. That has saved me a lot of trouble, advertising for a companion and hiring someone, and of course no one wants to come to an isolated valley in the middle of the mountains.'

Professor Madison was not so enthusiastic when he returned and Carolyn told him about it.

'Surely, after the way Don Carlos has revealed his feelings you don't want to go and live in his house,' he exclaimed.

'I don't, at least not particularly. But Elena—well—Elena is something special.'

'Well, all right. I won't raise any objections but for God's sake don't try Don Carlos too far, or you may find you get more than you bargained for.'

Carolyn smiled. 'I won't. I'll keep out of his way. And after all, it's only for a couple of weeks.'

But as she packed her suitcases that evening she wondered whether she was indeed making the biggest mistake of her life.

# CHAPTER SIX

CAROLYN rolled over in the softly-sprung bed and reaching to the bedside table she glanced at her watch. It was almost two o'clock, and she groaned. Was she never going to get to sleep? She turned on to her back and stared unseeingly up at the ceiling. This was the second night she had tossed and turned about and it simply would not do.

On her arrival at the hacienda she had been greeted excitedly by Elena who showed her to the room she was to occupy. Large, and luxurious, with a cream fitted carpet and pale pink curtains and covers, it was far different from the camp bed at the dig, and yet she had grown used to the hardness beneath her back.

On her first night she had thought it was the newness of her surroundings, but now, here she was, still awake on her second night. Her mind felt too active to sleep; maybe she was remembering that this was after all Don Carlos's house, and he would not be pleased to find her there on his return no matter how much Rosa protested.

She had not seen Ramon at all. She had arrived before dinner the previous day and had dined with Elena in the nursery. Then it was bedtime and the next morning Rosa revealed that Ramon had gone out for the day, up river, fishing. He was not back before dinner and again Carolyn felt slightly relieved.

She wondered if he was back now. She supposed he would be. She was not particularly looking forward to meeting him either.

She slid out of bed now, and pulled on a dark blue nylon housecoat wrapping it closely about her. She padded to the door and opened it, listening. There was no sound, the whole household was asleep. She came out of her bedroom and silently descended the staircase. Her cigarettes were in the library where she had been reading after dinner. She opened the door silently, and closing it, switched on the standard lamp by the door. Then she almost jumped out of her skin. Ramon d'Alvarez was lounging in a chair near the empty fireplace, an empty glass hanging lazily in his hand. He sprang up when she switched on the light, and this was what startled her.

'Carolyn,' he muttered, shaking his head. 'What are you doing down here?'

Carolyn sighed. 'I came for my cigarettes. They're here, on the table. I'm sorry, I'll leave you.'

Ramon stepped forward, putting out a hand. 'No, please, don't go.'

Carolyn bit her lip. 'I'd better, Ramon. It's late. If anyone found us here it could be misconstrued ... again!'

Ramon flushed. 'I know. I'm sorry about that day at the lake. I was a coward. I am sorry, really. I should have told you about Anna.'

'Yes, you should.'

Ramon came nearer. 'I didn't tell you because I was afraid you would stop meeting me,' he said, huskily.

Carolyn stared at him. In the subdued light he looked more like Carlos than ever. She felt her stomach churning suddenly.

'I would have,' she said, slowly, and then bent her head. 'I—I must go.'

'Stay and have a drink with me.'

'I think you've had enough already,' said Carolyn, frowning.

Ramon hunched his shoulders. 'I needed it. Do you remember you said you didn't agree with arranged marriages? Well, that's what mine is. And now I've fallen in love—for the first time in my life—with another woman!'

'Ramon,' she said, softly. 'Don't tell me this.'

'Why not? You must know it's you that I love.' His fingers curved round her wrist drawing her towards him. He was young and ardent and Carolyn felt a sense of compassion for him. She let him find her lips with his own and responded gently when he kissed her. But the touch of her warm body went to his head, and his arms tightened, and the kiss hardened into passion. Carolyn struggled to free herself now, pushing him away from her, aware of an aching longing that had something to do with Don Carlos.

'*En elnombre de cielo!* Have you taken leave of your senses, Ramon?'

The cold voice that had shaken them once before brought Ramon abruptly back to normality. Carolyn took advantage of his relaxed hold, and thrust him away from her, confronting Don Carlos with trembling limbs.

'*Señorita Madison!* What are you doing here in my house?' Don Carlos was absolutely furious.

Carolyn twisted her hands behind her back. 'Rosa, your sister asked me to come because Señorita Alfonso

97

has been taken ill. I am taking care of Elena.'

'Like hell you are! Are you also taking care of Ramon?'

'Carlos, for God's sake.' Ramon spoke now. 'I tried to tell you before but you would not listen. I love Carolyn. I don't love Anna. I want to be released from my engagement contract.'

'No!' Carolyn spoke involuntarily. 'Ramon, no! Not for me. I don't love you!'

'Oh, please!' Don Carlos sounded nauseated. 'Spare me the histrionics. Ramon, go to bed.'

Ramon stood firm. 'I don't care what Carolyn says, Carlos. I do not want to marry Anna.'

'Tomorrow, Ramon.'

Ramon looked at Carolyn, hoping she would deny what she had said, but she merely shook her head and said: 'Yes. Go to bed, Ramon. I am also going to bed.'

'Not yet.' Don Carlos closed the door after his brother and leant back against it, preventing her exit.

'Oh, not again,' exclaimed Carolyn, trying to keep calm. 'Let me go to bed. If you have anything to say, take it up with your sister in the morning. I told her you would not be pleased.'

'I will take it up with Rosa in the morning, have no fear. But I wish you to know here and now that you will be leaving in the morning, is that understood? You may spend the rest of the night packing your bags as far as I am concerned, so long as you are ready to leave at nine a.m.'

Carolyn felt a strange feeling of dismay in the pit of her stomach. Until now, no one had ever treated her in such a manner, and besides infuriating her it hurt too, badly. She stared at him through the haze of tears which were threatening to fall, and thought she had never hated any man so much. How could she have thought he was attractive? How could she have allowed herself to think of him while Ramon was kissing her? It was degrading. He deserved Louisa Morelos, no matter how cold she might be. His own emotions were distorted, anyway. How she longed to destroy that sardonic expression he wore. How she would love to have him pleading with her to stay. And if ever he should be attracted to her, how wonderful to scorn him, to make him pay for the way he had treated both herself and Ramon.

'Are you going to let me go?' she asked now, trying to sound aloof and detached.

'Eventually. How long have you been here?'

'Since the day before yesterday. How about you?' She sounded insolent again.

'I arrived back this evening, about eleven thirty. Ramon knew I was back. In fact we had an argument about you earlier on.'

'You did?'

'Yes. He has some mistaken idea that he can cast his responsibilities aside at the drop of a hat. Of course, he cannot.'

'Of course,' she mimicked him. 'Oh, let me go. You are just too square to be real. I must be dreaming all this, I really must.'

'It's no dream, Señorita, I can assure you.' He straightened and opened the door. 'You won't forget what I've said will you?'

'No, Señor. How could I forget?'

Carolyn walked past him, and then stopped and

looked up at him. 'You would never shirk your responsibilities, would you? You would never act like that! It would be almost human, and that would never do.'

She gathered up her skirts and ran to the stairs, half afraid he might try to prevent her again, but he merely stood watching her. 'What's wrong?' she taunted him. 'Are you paralysed? Or isn't it good taste to chase the nursery maid up the stairs, Don Carlos?'

She didn't stop any longer, but ran the rest of the way, feeling a bubbling excited feeling inside her which burst into dejection when she closed her bedroom door. Well, she thought, my visit was certainly short-lived. I might have known!

To her surprise Carolyn fell into a deep and dreamless sleep and did not awaken until Maria, the maid, brought her early morning fruit juice and coffee.

'What time is it, Maria?' she asked, drowsily.

'It is a little after eight, Señorita.' The maid looked disturbed. 'Don Carlos is waiting to speak to Señorita Rosa. Is it true that you are leaving, Señorita?'

Carolyn sniffed, and sat up. 'I guess so, Maria. How did you hear about it?'

'When Don Carlos is angry, everyone hears about it,' said Maria, simply. 'Will you have your breakfast with Señorita Elena as yesterday?'

Carolyn bit her lip. 'Yes, I don't see why not. Thank you, Maria.'

After the young maid had smiled and withdrawn, Carolyn slid out of bed, leaving the coffee untouched. She opened the jalousies and stepped out on to the balcony. It was a glorious morning, and as her bedroom overlooked the lake, the view was quite breathtaking. The water looked cool and inviting, with the bright greenery of the surrounding trees and flowers reflected in its surface. A faint mist veiled the tops of the trees still, but soon it would lift and the sun would be hot and brilliant. She sighed. It was a pity she was being made to leave. She would have liked to have stayed and her desire to do so was in no way connected with the conditions here as compared to those back at the encampment. She liked Elena, she liked Rosa, she even liked Ramon in an entirely sympathetic way. But Don Carlos was something else again.

She dressed with care, deciding that for once Don Carlos should see her in something other than trousers or disarray. She chose a brilliant cerise-coloured shift, made of tricel, which moulded the generous contours of her body and ended just below her knees. It left a long expanse of slender tanned leg bare, and she put heelless tan sandals on her bare feet. Her hair she combed into silky order, leaving it loose about her shoulders. She applied a colourless lipstick to her mouth, touched her dark lashes with mascara, and felt ready to face anything.

She left her cases ready to be carried down, and then descended the staircase to the ground floor. She walked along to the nursery suite where, in the small dining-room, Elena waited for her, her face pale and distraught. She clasped Carolyn's hand as she came in, and said: 'Is it true? Is it true? Are you being made to leave?'

Carolyn sighed. 'Oh, Elena, honey, you know how it is with your brother and me. We just don't agree on anything. Besides, he doesn't even like me. It was bound to happen. I told Rosa that when she asked me to come.'

Elena burst into tears. 'You said you would stay,' she sobbed, violently. 'You said you would *stay*!'

Carolyn exhaled loudly. 'Elena, don't cry, please. Señorita Alfonso will be better soon, and then——'

'I don't want her to get better,' Elena interrupted her loudly. 'I want you to stay with me.' She looked up at Carolyn with tearwet eyes. 'Please, Carolyn. It's you I want. Please, *please* stay.'

'Elena, I can't. If Don Carlos says I can't, I can't.' Carolyn sighed again. 'I'm sorry, darling. Look, I'll ask him if you can come to the site sometimes, to see me.'

'No. I don't want to come to the site. I want you to stay here. Carolyn, please!'

Carolyn was beginning to get disturbed. Elena was crying uncontrollably now, and her voice was getting higher and higher. She tried to calm her, but Elena just shook her off, accusing her of not caring whether she stayed or not.

Carolyn was at her wits' end, not knowing what to say to her. She felt horribly guilty. She would not have allowed Rosa to persuade her to come in the first place. She had known this would happen. If only Don Carlos had stayed away another week, it would have been easier she thought.

Elena was working herself up into an hysterical state, almost screaming with her disappointment, and Carolyn gathered her close to her, trying to calm her. But Elena fought her off, coughing and choking and almost making herself sick. For once Carolyn felt a sense of relief when Don Carlos did appear, accompanied by Rosa, who looked distraught herself.

'Elena!' he exclaimed, angrily. 'Stop this at once! You cannot always have your own way!'

Then his dark eyes turned to Carolyn, momentarily resting on her bare legs, before he resumed his remarks to his sister.

'Carlos, can't you see the child wants Carolyn to stay?' Rosa exclaimed impatiently. 'Heavens, where is the harm? Señorita Alfonso is far too old for Elena, anyway.'

'Keep out of this, Rosa,' snapped Carlos, his brilliant eyes flashing. 'If you had not—*invited* Señorita Madison here, this would never have happened.'

'Please, p ... p ... please, C ... Carlos,' stammered Elena, still sobbing. 'Let her stay. I don't ask for many things. *Please!*'

'It is impossible, Elena.'

'Why is it impossible?' Elena pressed a hand to her trembling mouth. 'Why are you so against it? Is it because Carolyn is not afraid of you as we are?'

'*Elena!*' It was Rosa who spoke now.

'I don't care, it's true! Carlos is making me pay because of his own silly pride!' Elena burst into loud sobbing again.

Carlos looked absolutely incensed, thought Carolyn, and she thought it was perhaps time she made a quiet exit.

'A moment, Señorita.' It was Carlos who spoke. 'Have you discussed me with my own sister?'

Carolyn's eyes widened. 'No. Of course not.'

Elena caught his hand. 'She hasn't, Carlos. It was me. Please, won't you change your mind?'

'No.' Carlos looked at Carolyn. 'Get out of my

house!'

Carolyn stared at him for a moment, unable to move, and then she turned and walked swiftly out of the door. At once she heard Elena scream, and then there was silence. She stood, motionless, and Rosa came dashing out of the room.

'Elena has fainted,' she said. 'Find Ramon. Ask him to get in touch with our doctor.'

Carolyn nodded and sped along the passage. She found Ramon in the dining-room. In as few words as possible she managed to convey the urgency of her request, and he nodded, and said:

'Okay. I'll take the helicopter. Tell Rosa I should be back within the hour.'

After he had left Carolyn walked back towards the nursery wing. She couldn't leave now, not without knowing that Elena was going to be all right.

Elena was conscious again, but still weak and frightened, and as Carolyn appeared Don Carlos lifted her into his arms and carried her past Carolyn, out of the room, and along the corridor.

'Carlos will put her in her room,' said Rosa, following him. 'Carolyn, what can I say? I feel I am to blame.'

'Don't be silly,' said Carolyn huskily. 'Will she be all right?'

'Of course. The doctor is merely a formality. She has fainted before. She works herself up into such a state that her body cannot stand it. This is the first time Carlos has been responsible. Usually it is I, or one of the servants who is to blame. Do not think we are stupid, Carolyn. We realise she can do this to get her own way, but on the other hand it is quite disturbing to realise how weak she still is. Doctor Fallone has said that in time she will be incapable of working herself up into such a state, and I must admit it is a long time since it happened. It is just that she has taken such an intense liking to you, and Carlos is thwarting her.'

Carolyn sighed. 'Well, if she's okay, I'd better get my things together. Can I—well—will someone run me back to the camp?'

'Wait,' said Rosa, firmly. 'Please, Carolyn, wait. I have the feeling that my brother may fall in with Elena's wishes yet.'

Carolyn felt disturbed in spite of herself. She wanted to say that she had no desire to stay on those terms, not in a house with a man who hated and despised her.

But instead, she said: 'All right. I'll have some coffee, here. You know where I am.'

Rosa squeezed her arm. 'Thank you, Carolyn,' then she too went upstairs.

Carolyn poured herself some coffee, helped herself to a cigarette, and drew on it luxuriously, savouring the relaxation it engendered. What a situation she had gotten herself into.

In a while her nerves calmed and she could think more lucidly. She could go, if she really wanted to. No one could force her to stay, and yet, she shook her head. Why did she want to stay? It wasn't only Elena's demands that drew her. It was a feeling of fury against Don Carlos, a longing to get even with him for the way he had treated her. But how could she do that? Unless ... Unless in some way she could disarm him, be less insolent towards him, less of a modern girl, and more of the kind of subdued female he seemed to like.

And then, when he was beginning to like her, turn that liking into something else. Make him want her; desire her; and then torture him as he had tortured her since she arrived in the valley.

Her lips curved in a wry smile. Such a task would not be an easy one. How could she subjugate her ideas to any man, much less a man she openly detested? She grimaced. Detest was the wrong word. She didn't detest him; she hated him, his arrogance, everything he stood for.

She was so engrossed in her thoughts that she had not heard anyone approaching and she almost jumped out of her skin when he spoke.

'Must you always do that?' she exclaimed, furiously, momentarily forgetting her thoughts of a few moments ago.

Don Carlos shrugged his broad shoulders. 'I merely said that the doctor has arrived. Ramon brought him.'

'I didn't hear the helicopter.'

'That is hardly surprising. You seemed lost in a world of your own.'

Carolyn acceded this comment with a nod of her head, and then got awkwardly to her feet. 'Well?' she said. 'Have you come to tell me the car is waiting for me?'

Don Carlos shook his head, and Carolyn was acutely conscious of the penetration of those dark eyes. He seemed to be studying her very thoroughly, and she felt a sense of frustration. Surely he would never look at a woman of his own race and class as he was looking at her now.

She turned her back on him abruptly, and walked

across to open french doors which led out into the cool shaded courtyard. 'For heaven's sake, say what you have to say and let me go,' she said, tightly.

'Why? Does my looking at you bother you?' His voice was strangely disturbing.

'It annoys me,' retorted Carolyn, swinging round. 'You seem to think you can treat me in any way you like and I cannot object.'

'How can you?' he asked, a muscle jerking at the corner of his mouth. 'You allow Ramon to kiss you, you hold hands with one of the geologists at your father's excavation, why should you object to my merely looking at you?'

Carolyn's eyes narrowed. 'How observant you are where I am concerned,' she taunted him. Then: 'Look, time is getting on. What is going to happen? I should like to know.'

'I have agreed with Elena that you shall stay until Señorita Alfonso is better, and not one day longer.'

'How kind!' Carolyn clenched her fists. 'And what if I refuse to stay? After all, you have been extremely unpleasant about the whole affair.'

Don Carlos stared at her. 'You will not refuse,' he commanded, angrily.

'Oh, won't I? And how are you going to ensure that?'

To her surprise he turned now, reaching for his cheroots and lighting one with hands that were not quite steady. Then he put it between his teeth and thrust his hands arrogantly into his trousers pockets. He was wearing tight-fitting brown pants and knee-length boots, and she thought he looked every inch the lord of the valley.

'Señorita, for eight years I have been the master here. I do not intend to be thwarted by a comparative stranger.'

Carolyn shrugged her slim shoulders. 'Maybe you would have more success if you used a little more discretion,' she said, angrily.

'If you wish me to plead with you now, you will be disappointed,' he returned, controlling his temper with difficulty.

Carolyn half smiled, knowing herself for once as the mistress of the situation. 'Then maybe you could persuade me,' she said, lazily. 'For example, Elena is obviously not going to be able to come down until lunch——'

'That is true. The doctor is giving her a sedative.'

'—so, where are you going?'

He frowned, his eyes curious. 'Why?'

'Well, I shall be bored, hanging about here alone, and as you don't wish me to spend time with Ramon, perhaps you could entertain me.' She spared a half-regretful thought for Louisa Morelos, and then continued with her plan, a demon inside her urging her on.

Don Carlos looked positively astounded. 'You cannot be serious, Señorita.'

'Why not?'

He shook his head, and she thought the task she had set herself was going to provide her with a great deal of entertainment in itself.

'I think the sun must have been a little hot yesterday,' he said, stiffly. 'I have no intention of taking you anywhere.'

Carolyn bent her head. 'Then I guess I had better

collect my bags——'

'*Damn you!*' he muttered, violently. 'What do you think you can do to me?'

'I think I can make you take me with you,' she said, walking towards him indolently. 'Surely I am not so repulsive!'

Don Carlos was breathing hard. 'Señorita, I warn you——'

'I'm listening.' She ran her tongue provocatively over her lips. 'Or should I go and get changed? I should hazard a guess that what I am wearing is hardly suitable for where we are going.'

He bent his head, and lifted his shoulders slowly. 'Very well, Señorita. Get changed, but be warned!' He looked up. 'You may find you have overstepped yourself.'

Carolyn felt a gurgle of satisfaction stirring inside her, and without another word she left him and went to get changed.

She dressed in navy blue stretch pants and an orange-and-white-checked shirt which she thrust into the waistband of her trousers. Then shedding the sandals for knee-length boots of mushroom-coloured suède she was ready. She descended the stairs swiftly, her dark glasses swinging from her hand. Don Carlos was waiting impatiently in the hall below, and watched her descent with narrowed eyes.

'I'm ready,' she said, smiling, and then biting her lip as Rosa appeared from the direction of the kitchen and looked in astonishment at them.

'*Qué?*' she exclaimed. 'Where are you going, Carlos?'

'To the farm,' said Carlos, shortly, and walked towards the wide arched doorway. 'Are you coming, Señorita?'

Carolyn's teeth held her bottom lip and she nodded in an amused fashion. Rosa stared at them. 'Señorita Madison is going with you, Carlos?'

'That is obvious,' returned Carlos. 'Come.'

Carolyn lifted her shoulders at Rosa and followed him. Outside the air was sweet, but very warm. It was getting hotter every minute. Carolyn thought regretfully that she should have had a hat, but she quickened her stride to keep up with Carlos as he strode ahead of her. They encircled the house to where a cluster of outbuildings nestled among the trees. Here the stables were housed, and Carolyn swallowed hard. It was years since she had done any horse-riding.

The stable-boy had a huge white stallion saddled in readiness, and Carlos quickly told him to prepare the brown and white mare for Señorita Madison. Carolyn found the mare, Anita, a quiet-eyed gentle animal, and she was thankful. She would not have cared to have been mounted on the stallion, Maximo.

Carlos did not look at her as he steered the stallion out of the yard, and across the stretch of cultivated grass to where the hard earth wound away along the mountainous walls of the valley in a rough track. It was this track that Carlos took, allowing Maximo his head as soon as the track levelled out. Carolyn urged Anita on, pressing her heels into the mare's sides and being rewarded by the easy canter she achieved. She had little time to admire the magnificent view of the lake below them, and the heat was tempered by a strong breeze which lifted her hair and tangled it into wild disorder. Her cheeks were flushed and her lips parted, and she thought she had never felt so completely happy.

Then they were descending a steep path which led down to where fields of cultivated land bore witness to someone's labours, and cattle grazed in the fields around a small, but attractive stone farmhouse. Horses were corralled in pens, and in another pen she saw some young bulls. Was this where Don Carlos bred the bulls for the arena? It was obviously the farm which supplied the fresh vegetables for the hacienda, and the milk and cream and cheeses.

Men were working in the fields, and in the yard near the house chickens scratched. It was more like a farm in England than anything, and Carolyn was amazed that this valley could hold so many contrasts.

She dismounted when Carlos did, not waiting for him to help her even had he been going to do so, and flexed her muscles rather tiredly. It had been a hard ride, and she was not used to it. A man came to greet them looking curiously at Carolyn, but merely addressing Don Carlos. He called him *padrone* and treated him with respect. Their conversation was wholly in Spanish and precluded Carolyn's inclusion. She glanced about her, and smiled when several men stopped to stare at her. This was better than relaxing in the garden at the hacienda, although now the sun was burning down on her head again.

As though aware of this Carlos turned and said: 'Come, we are going to the corrals, but first, I think, you need something for your head. Pancho's wife will lend you a sombrero.'

Carolyn noticed that he wore nothing on his head,

but he was used to the sun and it did not bother him. Even so, when he emerged he was carrying two hats, and thrust one on to the back of his own head as he handed Carolyn hers. She jammed hers down on her head, tightening the strap under her chin, and feeling quite ridiculous suddenly. But catching a glimpse of herself in the reflection in a nearby window she saw that she did not look bad at all. The hat was deliciously cooling, and protected the back of her neck.

As Carolyn followed Carlos across the field to the paddocks she felt like a child following its father. It was obvious he had no intention of paying any attention to her, and she compressed her lips angrily. Running she caught him up, and panting, she said:

'Is it illegal for a man like you to walk with a woman?'

He frowned. 'Now what are you talking about?'

'You know perfectly well. You have ridden ahead of me all the way here, ignored me on our arrival, and now you simply walk away and expect me to follow you. Is this the way you treat Louisa?'

Carlos halted, looking down at her angrily. 'Don't you mention Louisa's name,' he muttered. 'My relationship with Louisa is by choice, not by blackmail.'

'Oh!' Carolyn gasped, and would have slapped his face again, but he caught her wrist this time.

'I think not,' he said, violently. 'Now behave yourself, and behave like a young woman, not a spoilt baby!'

Carolyn wrenched her wrist out of his grasp, and felt like stamping her foot in annoyance. What was there about this man that brought out such horrible tendencies inside her?

The corrals they went to were those containing the young bulls. Carolyn leaned on the fence nervously, wondering what she would do if one charged her. It was a terrifying thought. Carlos spoke to the man in charge and he nodded and opened a gate allowing all but one of the bulls to escape into another pen. Then he closed it again, and Carlos vaulted over the fence into the corral with the bull.

'No!' gasped Carolyn in horror, as the bull snorted angrily and stood staring with malevolent eyes at Carlos.

But Carlos obviously had no fear. He walked slowly across the pen, taking his hat off and waving it in the bull's face provocatively. A crowd of workers were gathering round the pen, all willing for some free entertainment, and from the expressions on their faces Carolyn thought they had seen and enjoyed this before. Certainly the man in the ring bore little resemblance to the cool, aloof, and detached Spaniard Carolyn had grown used to seeing. He was cool certainly, and relaxed, but his expression was one of exhilaration and satisfaction, and when the bull pawed the ground he laughed and urged it on.

Carolyn became mesmerised. The bull grew impatient and began to move forward, gathering speed as it came. It ran close to Carlos, aiming for the wide sombrero in his hand. The men around the ring shouted *'Ole!'* excitedly, and the bull halted, bewildered, and turned to charge again. Carolyn had seen a bull-fight before, but this was not the cruel, mindless killing of a fine animal. This was a man pitting his wits against an animal equally as dangerous as himself. There were no picadors and banderillos here; only a matador with immense courage.

Carolyn lost count of the number of times the bull charged. It only seemed that every time the bull was closer to the man in the ring, and her stomach felt as though someone had installed a mixing machine. Then, as the bull tired, Carlos swung himself back over the fence and nodded to the chargehand.

'*Si*,' he said. '*Esta bien*, Gustavo.'

The man nodded also, and smiled as he spoke words of admiration. Carlos slid his hat back on to his head and looked at Carolyn. Her eyes met his and for a moment her limbs turned to water. Today his eyes were not guarded and the look in their depths caused her to turn away, her heart pounding heavily.

Then they were walking back to where their horses were tethered.

'This bull is for the bull-ring,' he said, in answer to her unspoken question. 'He is a fine animal, a brave fighter. He will do well.'

'And be killed,' said Carolyn, bitterly, trying to summon up the anger she had felt for him before.

'*Si*, and be killed.' He nodded. 'But it will be a brave and magnificent death, and what more could anyone ask?'

Carolyn shook her head. She felt disturbed and confused, her emotions aroused by the exhibition she had just witnessed. It had put Carlos in an entirely different light. She had thought him a man before. Now she was sure of it. And his attraction was a living thing that she could feel.

The man who appeared to run the farm and his wife had glasses of sweet fruit juice waiting for them on their return, and then they mounted their horses and waved goodbye.

It was very hot on the way back, and Carolyn was glad of her hat. They went a different way, along the valley floor near the river, where the flame trees grew in profusion looking exotic and luxuriant. They picked their way along tracks sometimes hidden by the overhanging greenery, until they came upon the shores of the lake.

Carolyn was still in a strange mood, unwilling to search for reasons for the troubled state of her emotions. Carlos was riding ahead, and she was shaken when he halted at the lakeside, sliding down off the white stallion and leading it to the water to drink. She sat still watching him and he turned and said: 'Water the horse, or are you cruel, too?'

Carolyn urged the horse forward, and Anita walked to the very water's edge and bent her head gratefully. Carolyn remained where she was, and Carlos lit a cheroot and looked at her through narrowed eyes.

'Well?' he said. 'Are you in such a hurry to get back?'

Carolyn flushed. 'It must be nearly lunchtime.'

'It's a little after twelve,' he said, glancing at the gold watch on his wrist. 'Get down!'

Carolyn shrugged, and lifted her foot over the saddle and slid down forwards. She looked at him swiftly, and then away again. He had unbuttoned his shirt almost to his waist, and the brown chest with its dark hairs disturbed her uncomfortably. She wondered whether Louisa ever saw him like this, or whether with her he was always formal, always immaculately dressed. She thought this was likely. Louisa was fastidious; she was not the kind of woman to find a man's body attractive unless it was perfectly garbed.

She walked away from him, to the edge of the bank and looked down into the clear water. The stones on the bottom could be clearly seen and she thought how delicious it would be to swim now, when her whole body ached for its coolness. She lifted the heavy weight of her hair to allow the breeze to caress her neck, and then dropped it again remembering that other time when Ramon had kissed her and Carlos had come through the bushes like an avenging angel. She half smiled at her thoughts as she turned and he said: 'So. What is amusing you now?'

'Nothing much,' she shook her head. 'Tell me, do you and Louisa ever spend any time alone together?'

'That is a personal question,' he said, his eyes darkening. 'Why do you ask?'

She shrugged. 'Well, you're so correct, I half thought you might require a chaperon, until you're married.' Her words were deliberately taunting.

His fists clenched. 'You are insolent,' he snapped, angrily.

'No, only curious,' she replied, amused at the way she could annoy him so easily. But it was a game she liked to play even though that look she had seen in his eyes at the corral still disturbed her.

Then she looked down and saw something large and black with long legs and a furry body on her bare arm. She gave a startled gasp and brushed it away, shivering. She looked up to find Carlos laughing now.

'It's not funny,' she exclaimed, hotly. 'What was it?'

'Just a fly,' he said indicating the unfortunate insect lying prostrate on the sandy ground at their feet. 'You are a strange mixture, Carolyn, half child, half woman!'

She stared at him. 'Am I, Carlos?'

He bent his head and stood on the end of his cheroot. 'Yes,' he muttered, shortly, and without another word lifted Maximo's bridle and climbed into the saddle.

Carolyn watched him and then shrugging she did the same, and when Carlos pressed his heels into the stallion's sides and he broke into a gallop she did likewise and followed him even though her whole body ached with weariness.

## CHAPTER SEVEN

CAROLYN did not see Carlos any more that day. He lunched alone in his study, and Carolyn shared her meal with Rosa, Ramon having mysteriously disappeared again. Carolyn suspected he had been told to do so by Carlos, but she at least was relieved. At least that unpleasant scene during last night had convinced her that she was not seriously interested in the younger Alvarez, and if he had been temporarily abashed by her attitude it was all to the good.

She spent a lonely afternoon and evening. Rosa had her own work to attend to and Elena was not permitted any visitors. The following morning therefore Carolyn was surprised when Elena herself came bouncing on to Carolyn's bed soon after seven, looking completely relaxed again, and obviously well pleased with the results of her hysteria the previous day.

'I thought you were never going to wake up,' said Elena, grinning cheekily. 'So I decided to hurry you up. It's a marvellous morning and now that you're staying we can plan what we are going to do every day!'

'Oh, really!' Carolyn rubbed her eyes sleepily. 'I gather you have no overhanging effects from your ordeal yesterday.'

'No. Why should I have? You're here, aren't you, and that was all I ever wanted.'

Carolyn grimaced wryly, and sat up. 'All right, Elena. But don't try any of those tricks on me or I'll walk out of here so fast you won't know I've gone.'

Elena pouted her lips. 'Don't be cross, Carolyn. You sound exactly like Carlos! I didn't put anything on, you know. I really do have those attacks.'

'Well, I'll keep an open mind,' said Carolyn, slowly. 'But I'll tell you frankly, if I were your brother and there was any doubt in my mind, I'd watch you like a hawk and the first time I had any suspicions that you might be fooling, I'd put you over my knee and give you a good spanking!'

Elena flushed. 'All right, all right! Now can we forget it?'

Carolyn shrugged, and slid out of bed. 'I suppose so.' She smiled. 'Shall we go for a swim?' She pushed open the shutters. 'Before breakfast?'

Elena hunched her shoulders. 'I can't swim. Carlos and Ramon have tried to teach me but I just haven't any confidence.'

'I see.' Carolyn drew out the black bikini and studied it with a half-amused expression on her face before returning it to the drawer. Instead she took out a one-piece grey-and-red-striped suit that was much more conservative in style. 'Do you have a swimsuit?'

'Ye-es.'

'Go put it on. I'll teach you to swim myself.'

Elena was reluctant but she went, glancing back over her shoulder as though expecting Carolyn to change her mind. But Carolyn was entering the bathroom to take a shower before donning the swimsuit.

When Elena met Carolyn on the upper landing she was wearing the most old-fashioned swimming costume Carolyn had ever seen. It was all black with thick wide straps and little shaping. It had a skirt which covered the upper half of her legs and with her pale face and black hair she looked terrible.

'Good lord!' Carolyn shook her head. 'Where did you get that monstrosity?'

Elena looked indignant. 'It was Rosa's. It's all right, isn't it?'

Carolyn made a moue with her lips. 'Depends what you are supposed to be dressed for. Oh, Elena, it's *ghastly*. You can't possibly learn to swim in something so confining. Come on, I have several swimsuits. I'm sure we can find one to fit you.'

Elena looked doubtful but when Carolyn produced a scarlet swimsuit edged with white braiding her eyes lit up and when Carolyn had helped her into it she stood in front of the dressing-table mirror turning from side to side admiring herself.

'It's beautiful!' she exclaimed, enthusiastically. 'Oh, Carolyn, can I really wear it?'

'You can keep it, if you like,' said Carolyn nodding. 'I don't wear it very often. I prefer a bikini in a two-piece, but I hardly think your brother will consider you old enough to wear such a thing!'

Elena laughed, and after collecting towels they made their way down to the swimming pool. The water was slightly warmer than the lake, the sun striking through the shallow end and Carolyn thought that at least Elena ran no risks of getting a chill in the pool.

Teaching Elena to swim was not the easiest thing in the world. Used as she was to getting her own way, she refused to listen to instructions and Carolyn got very exasperated with her.

'How do you expect to learn if you won't do as you're told?' she said, when Elena had panicked and swallowed several mouthfuls of water, causing her to choke alarmingly.

Elena looked at her through watering eyes. 'You've got no patience,' she accused Carolyn, angrily.

'Patience!' exclaimed Carolyn indignantly. 'You would try the patience of a saint!'

Elena's face puckered, and Carolyn raised her eyes heavenward. 'For goodness' sake, Elena,' she said, shaking her head. 'Don't be such a baby! If you don't want to learn, say so, and you can play here while I go swim in the deep end.'

Elena's expression became sulky. 'You're supposed to be here to take care of me!' she retorted.

'Oh, really!' Carolyn put her hands on her hips. 'Is that the kind of remark I am going to hear every time I don't agree with what you decide?'

'Probably!' The deep voice startled Carolyn and she looked up in surprise to find Carlos standing by the pool looking down at them. He was dressed in a towelling robe which hung loose over swimming shorts, and looked tanned and muscular, his dark hair attractively ruffled and covered in tiny drops of water. He must have been swimming in the lake, she thought, and felt disturbingly aware of his attraction once again.

Now she climbed out of the pool, and lifted a towel from the back of a lounging chair. She rubbed her hair and face, and lifted mocking green eyes to his.

'You would know, of course,' she said.

He inclined his head, equally as mockingly, and

Carolyn felt the hot colour run up her cheeks. He infuriated her and she looked down at Elena and said: 'Well? Are you coming out?'

Elena shrugged and climbed out. 'Carolyn soon gets annoyed,' she said plaintively to Carlos. 'I only wanted to stop a minute and show her how I can float against the side.'

Carlos shrugged also. 'Floating against the security of a handrail is not clever,' he said, easily. 'If Señorita Madison is attempting to teach you to swim, you should at least afford her your attention to show your appreciation, Elena.'

'Of course, you would say that!' retorted Elena. She sighed. 'I do want to learn, Carlos. It's just—I'm frightened!'

'And Señorita Madison? Has she swum today? Or have you kept her chained to your side?'

Elena screwed up her nose. 'I told you—she's been teaching me to swim!'

'In other words, no. Very well, Elena. Run indoors and get dressed. Señorita Madison may have a few minutes before breakfast, if she hurries.'

Elena looked about to protest, and then remembering what Carolyn had said earlier and seeing the look in her eyes, she heaved a sigh and marched away towards the hacienda.

Carlos looked at Carolyn then, his eyes appraising the red and grey swimsuit. Carolyn turned away, dropped the towel, and was about to enter the pool when Carlos said:

'Come: we will swim in the lake.'

'*We!*' echoed Carolyn, in astonishment.

'The lake is cooler,' he explained, taking her arm

and leading her across the lawns to where the steps led down to the lakeside. 'Naturally you will not swim in the lake alone. It is deep and dangerous. You could get cramp.'

'So could you,' she reminded him.

'I have swum in the lake since I was a child,' he said, coolly. 'It holds no fears for me.'

Carolyn was conscious of him with every fibre of her being, and when he shed the white towelling jacket she saw that although his body was lean without an ounce of spare flesh on him his back was smooth and muscular, and evenly tanned. It was a pleasure, just looking at him, but when those dark eyes turned on her she looked away swiftly and without waiting for him she leant forward and dived cleanly into the icy depths.

She came up gasping, but her body felt alive, invigorated, and she looked round for him bewilderedly. He was nowhere in sight. She felt a faint twinge of apprehension, and she swung round expecting to find him beside her in the water. Just when she was beginning to feel alarmed he surfaced yards away from her and she realised he had dived in and swum underwater towards the centre of the lake.

Relief flooding her being, she began to swim towards him, and he waited for her before doing a swift crawl back to the jetty. Carolyn swam after him again, feeling amused, but making for a spot several yards away from him. Now he swam towards her lazily, and when he reached her, he said:

'Very good! I half thought you might be one of these so-called swimmers whose bathing suit never gets wet!'

She laughed. 'Oh, I adore it,' she exclaimed, forgetting her antipathy for a moment. 'You must miss all this when you're away.'

'I do.' Carlos smiled. It was the first time he had smiled at her without derision and her heart pounded heavily in her breast. She had only to relax and allow the tide to carry her close against that hard chest and then what would he do? She shivered and at once he said: 'You're cold. Come on, it's not wise to stay in after you begin to feel cold.'

'I'm not cold,' she said, fervently.

Carlos studied her for a moment, and then he shook his head almost imperceptibly and with a lithe movement vaulted out on to the low jetty. He put down a hand to help Carolyn and with some reluctance she put hers into it. He jerked hard and she tried to jump as he had done. But she stumbled ignominiously and fell on to the stone landing. The weight of her fall momentarily unbalanced Carlos and he tried to save himself from treading on her by going down on one knee. He had a hand on either side of her as she lay there half laughing at her stupidity when she became aware that he was not laughing and there was a strange expression in his dark eyes.

'Carlos . . .' she said, tentatively, wanting and yet not wanting to break the spell.

With a savage exclamation he leapt to his feet, pulling her up almost violently. '*Dios!*' he exclaimed. 'You are not content with attempting to ruin my brother's life but you also attempt to ruin mine!'

Carolyn twisted away from him. 'What on earth do you mean!' she exclaimed angrily. 'I didn't ask you to come swimming with me! I didn't want to fall here!'

'Didn't you?' He sounded sceptical, and she gave him a furious look before running away, up the steps to where she had left her towel beside the pool. Once in her bedroom she gave way to the tears which had been threatening her eyes, locking the door, and giving herself up to the unsteady realisation that Carlos Fernandez Monterra d'Alvarez could hurt her more than any man she had ever known, and she didn't know why.

Much later, Carolyn realised that by behaving in such an outraged fashion she had played right into the hands of Carlos Fernandez Monterra d'Alvarez. He already considered her an ignorant product of a permissive society and by behaving like a shrew she was fostering that opinion. Besides, when all else had been discarded it had been obvious that despite his antagonism towards her he had been conscious of her as a woman for the first time, a desirable woman, and his anger had been caused by his realisation of this fact. Had she acted differently she might have achieved that which she sought: his humiliation and her own self-satisfaction.

And yet, as she combed her hair in front of her dressing-table mirror prior to going down to lunch, she wondered why that prospect gave her so little cause for pleasure. He could hurt her so easily it was no easy task considering what might lie ahead of her.

In the days that followed she saw little of her employer, if that was what he could actually be deemed when she refused to accept any payment for her services. She ate with Elena and Rosa and spent all her free time entertaining the younger girl. When a car was put at their disposal by Rosa she drove back to the encampment to see her father. Although he visited the hacienda she did not feel relaxed with him there and preferred the informality of the camp and its freedom of restriction. It was strangely like home, going back there, and she half wished she had refused Rosa's request in the beginning. Elena was a demanding child and although they saw little of Ramon Carolyn was conscious of his brooding gaze whenever they did so. He was polite and nothing more, and she could only assume that his brother had convinced him of the futility of his desires. She was grateful that Ramon did not force his attentions upon her, and yet, at the hacienda, there was really only Ramon to whom she could really talk. She could not confide her feelings or emotions to a child like Elena, and although Rosa was kind and friendly she was not the kind of girl to encourage confidences. Carolyn indeed hardly saw her. She seemed always to be busy but Carolyn thought she wasted a lot of time worrying over the antics of the servants when she could have been enjoying herself. She thought that possibly Rosa was using work as an antidote to the misery she must have felt at the disappearance of her fiancé.

She attempted to continue with Elena's swimming lessons in the pool. Elena seemed to be improving even though she still spent a lot of time clinging to the side, and even achieved four strokes alone one morning. The days passed slowly. Carolyn was happy most of the time, yet she still found her thoughts often with Carlos d'Alvarez, wondering how he spent his time, and wishing he would spend some time with

Elena and herself. Even though they invariably argued he was at least stimulating company.

Then one morning the sound of a helicopter overhead when none was expected caused Elena to visibly droop. They were stretched out on loungers beneath a shady umbrella on the lawns beside the pool and Carolyn shaded her eyes, looking up, and saying:

'Who is it?'

Elena grimaced. 'I expect it's Louisa,' she said, gloomily. 'Rosa told me yesterday she was coming.'

Carolyn frowned, feeling a faint fluttery feeling in the pit of her stomach. 'You didn't tell me!'

'Why should I? You would have only felt as depressed about it as I was, and I am depressed enough for both of us!'

Carolyn laughed now. 'Oh, honestly, Elena, she's not so bad, surely.' She bit her lip. 'After all, she is your brother's fiancée, and one day she'll be your sister-in-law.'

'I know.' Elena sighed. 'I wonder if Pepe and Antonia are with her.'

'Who are they?'

'Her younger brother and sister.'

'Oh yes. Car—your brother mentioned them once.' Carolyn nodded.

Elena studied her curiously. 'You were going to say Carlos, weren't you? Why didn't you say it, then?' She leant closer. 'You never did tell me what happened that day Carlos took you out riding. Rosa was very shocked. She said Carlos seemed angry about something and yet he still took you with him.'

Carolyn felt her cheeks burn. 'Nothing happened at all, Elena. We rode to the farm, that was all.'

'That was *all*!' echoed the younger girl. 'Don't you realise that Carlos never bothers with any women except Louisa? To even take you riding was a magnificent achievement on your part I would say.' She smiled slyly. 'Seriously though, Carolyn, how did you manage it?'

'You're far too curious,' said Carolyn drawing out her cigarettes, and casting about in her mind for something to change the subject. 'Do you like Pepe and Antonia?'

'They're all right.' Elena lay back in her chair. 'Do you think Carlos is interested in you? Sort of—well—in a purely sexual way!'

'*Elena!*' Carolyn was horrified. 'Whatever do you know of such things? Of course he's not interested in me!'

Elena shrugged. 'I read books,' she said, calmly. 'I know the facts of life, Carolyn. I know a man can desire a woman without loving her.'

'For heaven's sake, Elena!' Carolyn rose to her feet, thrusting her hands deep into her trousers' pockets. 'I'm quite sure your knowledge of these matters would fill an encyclopaedia, but just now I don't wish to hear your views!'

Elena pouted. 'Now you're being sarcastic, which usually means I'm getting too near the truth for a person's liking.' She slid off her seat also, looking at Carolyn with curious eyes. 'What's wrong? Have you realised that Carlos is far more interesting than Ramon?'

Carolyn's eyes widened in astonishment. 'What do you know about Ramon?'

Elena looked complacent. 'Everything, I suppose.

He used to meet you at the lake every day until Carlos found out and put a stop to it. Now he mopes about the place, avoiding you because Carlos says he must. He is to marry Anna Costilho, but he wants you.'

'Really?' Carolyn gave an exasperated shake of her head. 'Quite the amateur detective, aren't you? Is there anything you don't know?'

'Yes—I don't know how you persuaded Carlos to take you riding.'

'Oh heavens, this is where I came in,' said Carolyn, dryly, and turning she began to walk slowly back to the hacienda. She had no desire to meet Louisa Morelos for a second time wearing trousers.

Elena ran to catch her up, 'Are you mad at me now?'

'No, I'm not mad.' Carolyn shrugged. 'However, I think you should keep your opinions to yourself. If this Anna Costilho comes here she will certainly not want to be regaled with the kind of gossip you give me.'

'Anna? Oh, she's nice. You'd like her. She's only nineteen, and she plays with me.'

Carolyn reflected that maybe it would be a good idea if the Morelos children were staying for her to suggest to Carlos that she return to the encampment. After all, it was over a week since she came here and surely Señorita Alfonso would be better very shortly. Already Rosa had intimated that the old governess had been spending some time out of bed in her room, and maybe even Rosa had regretted her decision to agree to Elena's request for her presence.

She sighed. It was a complicated business, and over-riding it all was the disturbing knowledge of her own reactions to the arrogant man who owned the valley.

That evening Elena came to her with the news that as Louisa, Pepe, and Antonia Morelos were staying for several days, she, Carolyn, would be expected to eat with the rest of the family in the main dining salon. This room was seldom used, and Rosa, Carolyn, and Elena had usually eaten together in the small breakfast-room near the nursery quarters.

Carolyn hesitated before saying: 'Are you sure it wouldn't be more convenient if I ate in my room? Did Señorita Alfonso eat with the family?'

'No, Señorita Alfonso did not, but she is not the kind of person you are. She would have felt uncomfortable eating with us. She would have had nothing to say. As for you, of course you are expected. Carlos would be very annoyed if you disobeyed his instructions.'

Carolyn grimaced. 'Would he? Whose instructions are these? His—or another of your hysterical demands?'

Elena looked hurt. 'Really, Carolyn, it wasn't my suggestion. Besides, we would be an odd number without you.'

'Gee, thanks!' Carolyn flopped on to the bed. 'Honestly, Elena, you reduce everything to bare necessities, don't you? All right, I'll come. But just don't expect me to hang around afterwards like some lost soul.'

The choice of something suitable to wear caused Carolyn some misgivings. The extroverted sense of humour she possessed urged her to wear something completely daring and exciting and *unsuitable*, while the more introverted desire to show she could be equally as elegant and decorous as Louisa Morelos convinced her she should not fall into the trap of her own outrageousness.

So she chose a tunic of white embroidered cotton that while appearing simple breathed elegance and style, its short skirt drawing attention to the smooth tanned length of her shapely legs. She combed her hair back, looping it behind her ears leaving the curve of her neck bare. She looked young and yet soignée her tanned skin reacting favourably against the whiteness of the dress.

Nevertheless, she was still extremely conscious of herself as she went down the stairs, wondering what Louisa would be wearing, and whether she was any more pleasant than that day on the site. She had not seen any of the Morelos family since their arrival; lunch she had shared with only Elena and afterwards while Elena had her siesta she had driven over to the encampment to see her father. It had been pleasant seeing him and David and Bill, and enjoying some gentle teasing about her position at the hacienda.

Now, she crossed the wide hallway thoughtfully, and as she heard voices coming from the lounge she entered only to find it was Carlos and Ramon and they were arguing. As they were speaking in rapid Spanish she could not make out what they were saying but from their expressions it was not pleasant. She heard her own name mentioned which clarified it all. She coughed awkwardly, and immediately an uncomfortable silence fell. Then Ramon gathered his composure and walking forward, took her hand, disregarding his brother's intent gaze.

'Carolyn,' he muttered, 'you look marvellous!'

Carolyn dragged her eyes from Carlos's angry face

with difficulty.

'I'm sorry if I'm causing you a lot of bother, Ramon,' she said, her eyes softening involuntarily.

'You're not,' he hastened to say, shaking his head. 'I—well—I have told Carlos I can't possibly marry Anna feeling as I do about you. I know I've said this before, but I can't help it. I mean it!'

The words seemed to echo round the room, and Carolyn moved restlessly. 'Ramon, don't do this for me!' she exclaimed. 'You know I told you—it wasn't serious!'

Carlos moved forward. In a dark lounge suit he looked achingly attractive. 'Unfortunately, my brother is not used to the kind of morals practised in your country,' he said, icily.

Carolyn felt the softness inside her harden. 'You don't know anything about the morals in my country,' she said, coldly. Her eyes were brilliant with her anger. 'I used to think that Spaniards, Italians, French, Portuguese were all Latin races, with hot blood in their veins, not iced water! You've destroyed that illusion, Señor! It's obvious that you haven't the faintest idea of what emotion is! Just because I am human enough to have feelings, *failings* perhaps you would call them, don't think I am stupid! What Ramon is talking about is *love*! Get a dictionary some time, and look it up. You might find it enlightening!'

Ramon's expression was one of delight and admiration, while Carlos looked positively malevolent, his dark features giving him a Satanic appearance.

'You think you can speak to me like that!' he ground out, stepping forward, when suddenly a light feminine footstep on the hall halted him, and Louisa appeared in the doorway, her eyes darting round the group with some interest.

'There you are, Carlos, my darling,' she said, sweetly. 'What is going on? Is something wrong?'

Carlos controlled himself with an immense effort, and turning aside from Carolyn and Ramon, greeted his fiancée warmly. 'Nothing is wrong, Louisa,' he said, smoothly. 'Did you have a good rest?'

Louisa squeezed his arm. 'Of course, Carlos. I always do what you tell me.' She slanted a look at Carolyn, making the other girl wonder how much of their conversation had been overheard. Then Elena and the two younger members of the Morelos family appeared.

At fifteen, Antonia was tall and attractive, and much more friendly towards Carolyn than her elder sister. Pepe was boyish, wore short trousers despite his age, and seemed much younger than Elena. Carolyn could see why their company did not throw Elena into transports of delight. Although polite and well behaved, neither of the Morelos children seemed inclined to show any interest in games or pastimes, and seeemed content to sit and listen to their elders talking, a practice Carolyn abhorred.

There were eight for dinner: Carlos and Louisa, Ramon and Rosa, Pepe and Antonia, and Carolyn and Elena. They sat at the long polished table in the dining salon, lit tonight by silver candelabra, and used silver dishes and cut glass goblets for their wine. It was the first time Carolyn had eaten a long Mexican-style dinner, the courses dragging out over two hours. At the end, she was glad to escape into the library, only to find she had been followed by Ramon.

'Now, Ramon, this has got to stop,' said Carolyn,

exasperatedly. 'I mean, you know perfectly well the opinion your brother has of me. He will be sure to imagine I am encouraging you.'

'You are.'

'What!' Carolyn stared at him.

'Yes, Carolyn. Not consciously, perhaps, but you are so lovely, and tonight you go to my head like champagne. Did you wear that dress deliberately?'

'This dress?' she echoed, faintly.

'Yes. A white dress, a white bridal dress! Carolyn, I don't care what Carlos says, I must have you. For my wife!'

'Are we interrupting anything?' Louisa's voice broke into their exchange, and for the first time Carolyn felt relief at seeing her.

'No, no, nothing,' she said, awkwardly, aware of the lord of the valley, close behind Louisa.

'On the contrary,' said Louisa, persistently, 'I distinctly heard Ramon mention something about wanting a wife. He couldn't mean you, could he, Señorita, after all, he is already affianced to my cousin, Anna Costilho.'

Carolyn felt disgruntled. 'I'm sure you're perfectly aware of the situation, Señorita,' she said, shortly. 'If you'll excuse me——'

She brushed past them, her skin tingling as she touched Carlos's hand where it rested on Louisa's arm. She just wanted to escape, to get away from all of them, including Elena.

She left the house through the arched entrance to the courtyard, breathing deeply of the cool night air. It was another marvellous evening, she thought, and then wrinkled her nose when she saw heavy black clouds hanging over the lake. It seemed there might be another of those torrential showers later, and she hoped the work had been completed on the dam so that the site would not be affected to its detriment. Sighing, she descended the steps to the lakeside, walking along the path there thoughtfully. How much longer could she stand this verbal sparring with Carlos, and how much longer could she stand Ramon's persistent declarations of intent? She had not thought, when she came so light-heartedly to Mexico, to find herself involved in the kind of situation more naturally found in the cocktail lounges and drawing rooms of London society.

The boathouse door stood wide, and stepping gingerly round the entrance she peered inside. The rowing boat was moored alongside a small yacht which Elena had told her was Carlos's. The small boat looked inviting, and she wondered if she dared take it out on the lake. Here it would be too easy for someone to surprise her, and she had no desire for any more conversation this evening.

With firm decision, she stepped into the rowing boat, used the oars to manoeuvre herself out of the boathouse, and then began to row evenly out across the moon-splattered waters of the lake. Now and then a cloud crossed the moon, dimming the filtered light, and giving the place a wild and eerie appearance. She smiled at her thoughts. Who would have thought, back in London, that she would be rowing a frail craft across a deep and dangerous lake in the heart of the Mexican sierras, when the moon was high and a storm was brewing?

At the remembrance of the storm, Carolyn shivered

and it was then she felt a spot of rain. It was only one spot at first, but it was huge, and as she had had some experience of the intensity of these storms, she began to row a little faster.

Another spot followed, and then another, until the downpour had really started, and her face was wet, her hair loosened from its coiffure hanging in wet strands about her neck. She cursed herself for her foolishness, when the moon slid behind the clouds, only appearing occasionally as though to show her the way back. The shoreline had never seemed so far away when it was dry, but now it seemed to be receding and not nearing. Her arms ached, and her back ached, and she felt like bursting into tears of self-recrimination.

At last she neared the stone jetty, and with weary hands reached out to clasp the rail. She almost jumped out of her skin, when strong hands caught her instead, dragging her bodily out of the boat on to the jetty. The rain was absolutely pouring now, but in the grey light she vaguely recognised Carlos. He was taking off his jacket as he raged at her angrily.

'Crazy little idiot!' he muttered, furiously. 'Have you no idea of the dangers you run? There are currents in that lake which should not be played with on a night like this. Look at you, you're soaked to the skin!'

'Oh, please,' exclaimed Carolyn tiredly, 'don't start again.'

Carlos was thrusting his jacket round her shoulders as she spoke, looking down at her with eyes which she felt sure would be burning with anger. He was wet, too, his thick silk shirt clinging to his skin.

'Come: we will run,' he commanded, taking her

wrist in hard fingers.

'The boat,' began Carolyn.

'The boat can be rescued in the morning. Come!'

Carolyn shook her head. 'You go,' she said, weakly. 'I haven't the strength!'

'*Dios*, you are exhausted,' he exclaimed, and then with decision he lifted her bodily into his arms and carried her to the comparative dryness of the boathouse. There he set her on her feet, and with deft movements erected a kerosene lamp and lit it with his lighter. In the faint glow they both looked wet and bedraggled, Carlos's hair clinging to his scalp, his shirt moulding the muscular width of his shoulders. Carolyn began to shiver, as much from nervous excitement as cold, but Carlos saw her and at once came to her.

'Why did you do it?' he ground out, in a tight voice.

'Do what? Go out on the lake? Oh, I don't know. I wanted to be alone.'

'Alone? For what? To consider your answer to Ramon's proposal?' His voice was harsh.

'Of course not,' she flared, stung by his tone. 'I don't want to marry Ramon. Why won't either of you realise that?'

'Why not? Is the brother of Don Carlos d'Alvarez not good enough for you?'

Carolyn gave a gasp. 'Oh, really,' she cried, 'what a ridiculous question, particularly after your attitude!' She stumbled to the door of the boathouse. 'I won't stay here and listen to you any longer,' she said, shaking her head, but Carlos's hard fingers curved round the back of her neck, gripping tightly, hurting her and successfully preventing her escape.

She moved her head trying to get away, but he was

close behind her, his other arm curving round her body drawing her back against him. She could feel the heat of his body through his wet clothes, and a trembling sensation invaded her lower limbs. She struggled at first, but when she felt the burning touch of his mouth against her neck she felt all resistance ebb out of her. He twisted her round savagely and his mouth sought and found hers.

The fury of the storm was all about them, a crash of thunder almost directly overhead seemed to shake the solid wooden boards of the boathouse. The rain pounded on the roof, the lake was whipped to a frenzy outside, while brilliant slashes of lightning rent the sky. Carolyn was hardly aware of anything except Carlos in those first few moments; the hard demanding pressure of his body, the violent passion of his mouth as they clung together, their shadows moulded into one.

As Carlos's kisses lengthened into mounting passion, Carolyn became aware of the knowledge that his passion was as much incensed by anger as emotion, he was hurting her deliberately, using his undoubted expertise to reduce her to complete submission, somehow proving to himself that he had been right about her all along. A shudder ran through her body, and with a superhuman effort she wrenched herself out of his arms, taking him by surprise where there had once been urgent response.

She gave a choked sob as with blazing eyes he attempted to grasp her wrist to pull her back into his arms. God, she thought shakily, I want to go back there, I want him to go on making love to me, and I don't particularly care whether he means it or not!

But she shook her head, breathing deeply, and without a backward glance she turned and ran out into the pouring rain. The ache in her arms and back was temporarily numbed by her emotions, and she fled sobbing up the steps and across the turf and into the house. Praying she would meet no one she reached the stairs, and with a supreme effort, the sanctuary of her room. She turned the key in the lock and leaned back against it, closing her eyes in agony.

After a few minutes she staggered across to the bed, flinging herself on her stomach, her tears drying on her cheeks as she felt bereft of all energy. A heavy sigh escaped her as she stared unseeingly into the soft pile of the carpet. At last she had realised what had been becoming painfully obvious for the past few days; the reason Carlos Fernandez Monterra d'Alvarez could hurt her so badly was simple: she was *in love* with him. She groaned. In love with a man who despised her, who thought her wanton and careless of emotion. How he must be amused to discover she was not indifferent to him at all! Would he discuss her with Louisa? How stupid she had been to imagine she could subdue the arrogant lord of Zaracus. Instead she had merely succeeded in subduing herself!

# CHAPTER EIGHT

THE following morning Carolyn found it terribly difficult to get up to face the day ahead. She had spent an almost sleepless night, torturing herself with her thoughts, unable to think of anything but trying to find a way to leave the hacienda at once.

When the maid brought her early morning fruit juice she questioned her about Señorita Alfonso's condition.

'She is much better, yes,' replied Maria, 'but I have heard talk that maybe she will return to her sister in Mexico City for a little holiday.'

'*No!*' exclaimed Carolyn, urgently. 'I mean,' as the maid's eyes grew curious, 'I only agreed to come here temporarily, until the Señorita was better. I—well—my father misses me and I should like to return to the encampment as soon as possible.'

Maria shrugged, eloquently. 'Perhaps Don Carlos will be able to tell you what has been decided,' she said, frowning, and Carolyn felt annoyed with herself for having said so much to one of the servants. Very likely Maria would derive great pleasure from relating their conversation to the rest of the staff and heaven knew what construction they might put on her words.

After the maid had gone, Carolyn showered and dressed in pants and a sleeveless sweater. Then she descended the stairs in search of Rosa. It was still reasonably early and so it was with surprise that she encountered Louisa Morelos in the small breakfast-room. Dressed in a chiffon négligé over a nightgown of a deeper shade of green she looked cool and beautiful, her eyes resting on Carolyn with no small degree of satisfaction.

'Ah! Señorita Madison,' she said, smiling. 'Won't you sit down?'

Carolyn shook her head. 'I—er—I'm looking for Rosa, Señorita.'

'Nevertheless, surely you can spare me a few moments,' remarked Louisa, paring a fresh peach delicately.

Carolyn thrust her thumbs into the waistband of her pants. 'You have something to say to me, Señorita?'

'Yes, just a few words. Sit down! You make me feel at a disadvantage towering over me like that.'

Carolyn felt sure Louisa would never allow herself to feel at a disadvantage, but she shrugged her slim shoulders and subsided into the seat opposite the Mexican girl. Louisa continued to pare the peach, stopping now and then to place succulent pieces into her small curved mouth. Then she wiped her hands on the table napkin, took a dainty sip of her coffee, and said:

'Just how did you manage to insinuate yourself into this household, Señorita?'

Carolyn gasped. '*Insinuate myself!*' she exclaimed.

'Yes. That is correct. When I visited with Carlos some short while ago you were living at the excavation site, now I return and find you installed in the hacienda in some ridiculous position as companion to Elena.'

Carolyn guarded her tongue and controlled her temper. She would not allow Louisa to get under her skin. 'Señorita Alfonso, Elena's governess, caught an unexpected chill,' she said coolly. 'Rosa asked me if I would take her place, temporarily, until the Señorita Alfonso is recovered. That is the position, Señorita Morelos.'

Louisa studied her pink fingernails. 'I see. But your position here seems to be—shall we say—a nebulous one.' She hastened on. 'That is to say, you eat with the family, you appear to use the facilities available to the family, and generally act more like a visitor than a servant!'

Carolyn bit on her lip, trying to retain her detachment. 'I am not a servant, Señorita,' she said, tightly. 'I do not accept a salary. I am doing this merely as a favour to Rosa, and of course to Elena.'

Louisa inclined her head slowly. 'I see,' she said again. 'However, I would prefer some other arrangement to be made. Señorita Alfonso is old, and unreliable. It is time she was permanently replaced by a younger person. Not someone as young as yourself, of course, but a responsible middle-aged person who would be capable of giving Elena lessons until she is well enough to return to school, which should not be so long now.'

Carolyn found this easier to accept. In fact if Louisa insisted on this it would solve all her immediate problems. Why then, for all she knew that staying at the hacienda could only bring heartache and misery, did she feel so antagonistic towards this woman? Of course, she was Carlos's fiancée, and as such Carolyn could not expect to feel friendly towards her, but there was something else about Louisa Morelos. A kind of malicious arrogance, that would not accept the presence of a girl of another race as anything more than an insult. Who was determined to reduce Carolyn to something so small she would be able to tread on her with her delicately shod foot, grinding her into the ground. Why should Louisa feel this way? Carolyn couldn't imagine, unless she thought that perhaps the English girl might provide a distraction for Carlos as well as for his younger brother. Carolyn almost smiled at the thought. If Louisa were really aware of what Carlos thought of Carolyn she would be jumping for joy.

But now Carolyn merely said: 'Is that all, Señorita?' with cool politeness.

'Not entirely,' said Louisa, her eyes narrowed as she surveyed the other girl, appraisingly. 'Tell me, what is your attitude towards my fiancé?'

'My attitude towards your fiancé?' echoed Carolyn, blankly. 'I—I don't think I understand you, Señorita.'

'Oh, I think you do, Señorita.' Louisa ran the tip of her tongue over her red lips. 'I think you understand very well indeed. It does not require a fortune-teller to reveal that you are attracted to him.'

'*What!*'

'Do not deny it, Señorita. I am not blind. And when the small Elena saw fit to enlighten me about your visit with him to the home farm, and subsequent other small meetings between you, my suspicions were confirmed.' As Carolyn felt the hot colour surge annoyingly into her cheeks, Louisa continued: 'It is apparent that having ensnared, only temporarily I am sure, the attentions of Ramon, you now seek to attract my fiancé. Am I not right?'

Carolyn stared at her, getting to her feet with

restless movements. This was just the sort of situation Elena would have envisaged might happen, and she felt a surge of anger towards the child. How dare she place herself, Carolyn, in such an invidious position?

'I think, Señorita, that you ought to take this matter up with your fiancé, not me,' snapped Carolyn, hiding her emotional disorder behind an attempt at attack.

'That will not do, you know, Señorita Madison,' retorted Louisa, her claws beginning to show. 'As an honourable man my fiancé would not seek to embarrass you by asking you to leave.'

'Oh, wouldn't he?' Carolyn gave a short laugh. 'It might interest you to know, Señorita, that I am only here because Elena worked herself up into such a state that she actually fainted and a doctor had to be called. Your *honourable* fiancé was forced into a situation he neither liked nor wanted. And as you're so keen on listening to Elena's gossip, perhaps you ought to take it up with her.'

'How dare you speak to me like that!' Louisa was furious now, all efforts to hide her anger forgotten. 'Just who do you think you are? It's obvious that until now you have never been in the company of people who know something about class and etiquette, and the right thing to do——'

'Oh, don't give me that!' gasped Carolyn. 'I've known guttersnipes with more idea of the right thing to do than your so-called society——'

'*Enough!*' The hard masculine tones brought both girls round to face Don Carlos. 'You are both behaving like guttersnipes! What on earth is going on?'

'You ask me!' Louisa fanned herself with her handkerchief faintly. 'I have never been so insulted in all my life!'

Carolyn's brilliant green eyes met Carlos's enigmatic dark ones. She could read nothing in their depths, and she could hardly believe that only twelve hours before he had been holding her in his arms, making violent passionate love to her, when now he looked as cold as a glacier and twice as hard. Oh yes, she thought wearily, Louisa was right in some ways; she had tried to attract Carlos, but only to hurt him, and in so doing had hurt herself, and indeed she had never met a man who could inflict such cruelty without the flicker of an eyelash.

'What have you been saying?' he asked, in a cold voice, making Carolyn shiver a little with the angry intensity of his gaze.

Carolyn lifted her shoulders. 'You ought to ask your fiancée that question. I didn't start this, she did.'

Carlos looked at Louisa. 'Well?'

Louisa gathered a little of her composure. 'Señorita Madison was rude and insulting,' she said, looking at Carlos with caressing eyes. Obviously, she was well aware of the most subtle way to gain Carlos's favour. She hesitated, gaining all attention to herself. 'Elena —Elena in her innocence told me how Señorita Madison had insisted that you take her with you on your visit to the farm——'

'Elena told you *what*!' Louisa drew back from the anger on Carlos's face.

'How—how Señorita Madison went with you to the farm.'

'So? What is wrong with that? It was a perfectly innocent excursion. Nothing happened of which I need to feel ashamed.' Carlos stubbed out the cheroot he had been smoking in a nearby ashtray. 'It seems to me, Louisa, that Elena has been attempting to make mischief, as usual, and you have played into her hands by tackling Señorita Madison.'

Carolyn's eyes widened. This couldn't be Carlos Fernandez Monterra d'Alvarez defending *her*!

Louisa looked a little disturbed. 'But, Carlos, what was I to think?' she exclaimed, petulantly. 'After all, you know very well how you would feel were I to pay calls with—well—other attractive men. I was jealous, and as I felt sure you would not have done this thing without duress...' Her voice trailed away. 'How was I to know you invited the Señorita to join you?' Her eyes were calculating now, studying Carolyn's face as though forcing her to some admission of guilt even were it only in the heightening of colour in her face, a different expression in the English girl's eyes.

Carlos looked impatient. 'Well, now you know, Louisa, what are you going to do about it?'

Louisa gave a startled ejaculation. 'Do about it? Why, Carlos, what do you mean?'

Carlos ran a hand round the back of his neck, flexing his muscles tiredly, and Carolyn wondered whether the soaking he had received the night before was responsible for the lack of patience and finesse he was using this morning. 'Louisa, what do you want me to say?' He sighed. 'Good God, surely we trust one another!'

Louisa approached him, running her fingers up the bare tanned skin of his forearm where the sleeves of his shirt were rolled back. The expression in her eyes was blatant and possessive, and Carolyn turned away nauseated. 'I want to leave here, Señor,' she said, in a tight little voice. 'Today.'

She glanced round indifferently, a gesture which required all her self-control, and surprised a look of satisfaction on Louisa's perfectly moulded face. But Carlos did not look satisfied, instead he seemed angry, and in scathing tones, he said:

'What is wrong? Has the task you so light-heartedly set yourself become too much for you to handle?'

Carolyn felt incensed. How dare he stand there asking questions of her reason for leaving, knowing the disgraceful way he had treated her only the night before? 'There have been—certain incidents, yes,' she said, coldly, 'which I found—how shall I put it?—too much for me to handle. Besides, I don't like the company here!' And with that childishly insulting remark she marched out of the room.

In her room she thrust all her belongings into her suitcases, and without calling for any help humped them down the staircase. Exhausted, she looked around the hall desperately. Surely Rosa would appear and alleviate any more unpleasant scenes. But when someone did appear it was Ramon, and he looked positively horrified to see that she intended leaving.

'But you can't,' he exclaimed, shaking his head. 'Not now.'

'What do you mean, not now?' Carolyn was in no mood to be persuaded by the man who had set most of these events in motion.

'Well, Anna is coming tomorrow.'

'Anna? You mean Anna Costilho, your fiancée?'

'The girl Carlos expects me to marry,' he corrected her.

'The girl you *will* marry,' retorted Carolyn, cynically. 'Look, Ramon, if anything could have persuaded me to leave sooner that would be the thing. After all, I am heartily sick of being treated like some cheap adventuress, out for any man who's willing and available.' She shook her head. 'When I came to Zaracus I thought I knew about life, but lord, how wrong can any one person be? I've never met such antagonism and maliciousness in all my life. Let me get back among English people, people I know and like, and who at least live open lives, not the kind of medieval intrigue you practise here!'

'But Carolyn——'

'But nothing. Just get me a car, or I swear I'll walk back to the encampment!'

Ramon was forced to do as she asked, and a few minutes later a chauffeur collected her cases and installed her in the back of a low black limousine. She breathed a sigh of relief as the dust swept round the car at their departure, and she settled back to try and regain some of the self-respect she had always thought she possessed.

The rest of the day passed reasonably calmly. Professor Madison was glad to see her back and mercifully did not ask too many questions. He had not been pleased to see her go, and merely welcomed her back without reservation, giving her time to collect her thoughts before discovering the reasons. The rest of the men gave her casual greetings, and within six hours Carolyn could almost believe she had never been away, and only the memory of a hard demanding body and a mouth which drove all thoughts of escape out of her mind, reminded her of the hacienda, and Louisa, and Elena.

The following morning a helicopter overhead heralded the arrival of the Costilhos. Only Carolyn was aware of this though, and she did not reveal her knowledge to her father as it would have prompted too many awkward questions. She took up her job again of typing out the reports and almost enjoyed being free to follow her own pursuits. But she did not go to the lake, even though she longed for the submersion in the cool water.

It was two days after her return to the encampment that a low sleek convertible purred across the camp site as she sat typing in the office. She slid off her stool, smoothing her hair automatically, to find herself confronted by a tall dark Spaniard with greying hair, blue eyes, and a warm and friendly expression. He was accompanied by a girl Carolyn had never seen before and Elena. Her eyes narrowed. What now? Her father was away at the dig and apart from José she was alone.

'Yes?' she said uncompromisingly.

The man smiled, and she thought he was most attractive. Probably in his late forties he could only be Manuel Costilho, and the girl must be his daughter, Anna.

'You must be Señorita Madison,' he said, holding out his hand in greeting.

'Yes, she is,' said Elena, nodding, and grinning at Carolyn irrepressibly.

Carolyn shook hands, and then said: 'And you're Señor Costilho, I guess.'

'That is correct. I am Manuel Costilho, and this is

my daughter, Anna.'

Carolyn smiled at the younger girl, and wondered uneasily what this was all about.

'You will be wondering why we are here,' said Señor Costilho, nodding. 'It is quite simple really. Elena wanted to see you and we agreed to drive her. Carlos and Louisa are away for the day in Oaxaca, so we were at a loose end.' He chuckled. 'That is what you English say, is it not?'

'Yes,' said Carolyn slowly. 'And—er—Ramon?'

Anna Costilho moved forward. She was like Louisa, small and dark and pale, but much gentler, and obviously more friendly. 'Ramon is at home, at the hacienda,' she said, now. 'He has told me about you, and I wanted to meet you for myself.'

'What!' Carolyn's composure fled. 'Oh, but—I don't know what he has said, but——'

'Do not alarm yourself, Señorita,' said Manuel Costilho, shaking his head. 'Ramon is an honest young man, and he has told Anna he does not feel he can marry her at this time because he is in love with you.' He spread wide his hands. 'This is not an unusual situation, Señorita. Very often our young men rebel against the restrictions placed on them by their elders, and very often they—how do you say it?—sow their wild oats elsewhere. I did this myself. But when marriage is arranged, and their final accounts are paid, they discover that the one their parents chose for them is usually the best.'

'You mean you think Ramon will eventually discover he wants to marry—Anna?' Carolyn stared at him.

'Of course. You did not take him seriously, Señorita?' His expression was anxious.

'No.' Carolyn shook her head. 'No. But even if I had, you are telling me that he is merely suffering from infatuation.'

'*Dios!*' Manuel Costilho laughed. 'This is a strange conversation to be having within minutes of our meeting, but yes, this is what I do mean. He may actually love you, but love is for long nights of passion, not for the cold light of an early dawn.'

Carolyn felt bewildered. This man actually believed this. She had to ask: 'And Carlos? His marriage is—the same?'

Manuel shrugged. 'Louisa has known Carlos since they were children. They would have been married many years ago were it not for the unhappy accident to Carlos's parents. When he had to assume control of the family things were delayed, you understand.'

Carolyn clenched her fists. It was barbaric! She could not believe that in this day and age people actually adhered to this kind of philosophy. If the Indians in the jungles still conducted their lives as they had done hundreds of years ago, then these arrogant Spanish descendants were equally as retarded socially. They actually believed that arranged marriages were the only sure way to success! She felt sick and bewildered by it all. Recovering her manners, she said: 'Perhaps you would like some coffee, Señor?'

Manuel Costilho nodded calmly. 'Yes. That would be delightful. Señorita Madison, please, do not look so concerned. I understand what youth is, how confused one's emotions can be. It is naturally not pleasant for a girl as—charming as yourself, to discover that her admirer is merely playing the game his ancestors have played for many, many years. You are a visitor here. You cannot expect to understand all our customs. They probably seem very primitive to you, coming from England. I know London very well, I was educated in Oxford and spent many months exploring your capital city. Nevertheless, I do not condone the attitudes of the young people there who seem to imagine marriage is something to wear for a while before casting it off in favour of something else in the cold light of a divorce court.'

Carolyn stiffened. 'There is a happy medium, Señor,' she said, coolly. 'Marriage in England can be as successful there as anywhere else. We do not all indulge ourselves to excess as you seem to imagine.'

Manuel Costilho laughed again. 'You see, you do not like me to criticise your way of life, because I do not understand it. Therefore you must not object to our way of life because you do not understand it.'

Against this argument Carolyn had no defence, but she felt suspiciously like a guinea pig, on display, and felt certain that Manuel Costilho had not felt so sure of Ramon or he would not have taken the trouble to drive out to the encampment to meet the girl Ramon was interested in, and calmly go ahead and tell her that he had no qualms about Ramon's eventual agreement to his arranged marriage. *Methinks he doth protest too much*, she thought to herself with some cynicism, and served the coffee with a little more enthusiasm. Still she continued with her self-catechism, it would be as well if Manuel Costilho was right. She had no particular desire to break up anyone's marriage, much less that of a nice girl like Anna. She would probably make Ramon the perfect wife, bear him fine sons, and care for his home. And if ever he was tempted to seek a stronger kind of relationship she would probably turn a blind eye to any indiscretions on his part. Carolyn accepted a cigarette from Anna's father with some distaste; that was something she could never accept, a man who was unwilling to remain faithful to his wife, and she thought that if ever she got married, which seemed unlikely in the light of her feelings for Carlos Fernandez Monterra d'Alvarez, she would make certain she was loved for herself alone.

She wondered idly what Carlos would say when he discovered they had been visiting the encampment, and what construction he would put on it all. Elena would no doubt make sure that he was informed, and he would probably feel a sense of satisfaction that someone else beside himself thought it necessary to enlighten her about the facts of the Spanish way of life.

# CHAPTER NINE

WITHIN three days Carolyn had decided to go home. Life in the valley was impossible now; the knowledge of Carlos and Louisa only a couple of miles away preparing for a marriage which seemed to hold nothing of the warmth and sincerity Carolyn had always thought necessary for complete happiness depressed her utterly, and although she had no illusions that the lord of Zaracus might be interested in herself, his actions on the night before she left the hacienda had proved to her that he was very much a man, with a man's appetites, which Louisa seemed incapable of assuaging. He had used her, as no doubt in the years to come he would use other women, to release the build-up of emotion he was bound to feel. It was horrible, and Carolyn could bear it no longer. She wanted to go back to England, to her home there, where at least people were what they appeared to be.

Professor Madison was half regretful, half relieved. He was aware that Carolyn had changed since she came to Zaracus and he did not want her to be hurt. He didn't know which of the Alvarez brothers was responsible, but one of them had taken the lighthearted lilt from her voice, and the quick, impetuous vitality from her actions. So he put aside his own feelings, and helped her to make the necessary arrangements.

It was settled that Bill should drive her back to

Veracruz where she would be able to pick up a flight to Mexico City, and from there back to London. The night before she was due to leave, Carolyn felt a sense of loss, as though by leaving the valley she would be merely transporting her physical body from this place while all her emotions and sensibilities would remain, locked forever in Zaracus.

Casting these thoughts aside, she went for a walk with David, trying to capture some feeling of excitement at her premature return to England. David, aware of her preoccupation, said, with some perception:

'It's Carlos d'Alvarez, isn't it?'

Carolyn stared at him, her cheeks flushing. 'It's Carlos, what?' she asked, deliberately misunderstanding him.

David heaved a sigh, kicking a stone moodily. 'You don't have to pretend with me, Carolyn, I knew probably before you knew yourself.'

Carolyn opened her mouth to deny it, and then hunched her shoulders dejectedly. 'Is it so obvious?'

'To me.' David pulled out his cigarettes, and lit two, handing her one. 'Why, Carolyn, that's what I want to know? Why?'

She drew on her cigarette, blowing smoke rings into the air. 'I wish I knew,' she said, lifting her shoulders helplessly. 'He's never given me a moment's encouragement.' She bit her lip. 'In fact quite the opposite. He never wanted me in his house, and once I was there I was only tolerated because Elena threw a tantrum when he insisted I should leave.'

David uttered an angry exclamation. 'Who does he think he is, anyway?' he muttered. 'Just because he's got money——'

'Oh, it's not that, David,' said Carolyn, shaking her head. 'I—well—I guess I understand him better now than I did before. It's a kind of hauteur he possesses. This complete detachment from the twentieth century, except in so far as his creature comforts are concerned. I don't fit in with his ideas of what a woman should be. In their society the woman they marry must be of aristocratic birth, with the right connections, and be prepared to submit entirely to authority. Outside of this rigid convention they have what we would call extra-marital activities. Love just doesn't enter into it!'

David let out his breath in a low whistle. 'What a situation!'

'Yes. It is, isn't it?' Carolyn nodded, trying to thrust down the threatening pangs of emotion she was feeling just talking about Carlos's affairs. 'Anyway, that's the way it is, and I want no part of it.'

David put an arm about her shoulders. 'And there's no reason why you should. Carolyn, you know perfectly well you have only to lift your little finger and I'll go up there and put my fist down his aristocratic throat!'

Carolyn allowed a small chuckle to escape as she remembered the day she had accompanied Carlos to the bull-pens, and seen his lithe and powerful body in action. She didn't think David, for all his good intentions, would stand a chance of socking Carlos Fernandez Monterra d'Alvarez on the jaw.

'And if you did that, the whole expedition would be destroyed,' she said, now, humouring him.

'So what! I wish I was coming back to London with

you. I've had just about enough of this place, now you're leaving.'

Carolyn shook her head. 'Dad is loving it, and you know it. Besides, secretly, you'd hate to give up all you've been working for.'

David looked disgruntled. 'Oh, maybe I would, maybe not. So, this is your last evening. How about a trip to the lake?'

Carolyn smiled, but shook her head slowly. 'I don't think so, David. That would really be asking for trouble.'

David looked annoyed. 'Why? What does it matter what happens now? You're leaving tomorrow anyway, so there's no fear of us becoming involved with one another, is there?'

'No—but—oh, it's no good, David. I'm not in the mood for swimming. Besides, I've packed my bathing suits.'

'Who said anything about swimming?'

'Well, anyway, swimming or not, I don't think so, thank you.'

David turned away in disappointment, and then the lights of a car swept the encampment as the low car from the hacienda drove across the site. Carolyn stiffened, and David sensing this looked at the car's occupant.

'Relax,' he said, moodily. 'It's not the lord of the valley.'

Carolyn looked at David curiously, and then at the car. The chauffeur who had driven her back from the hacienda was getting out of the car and looked about him frowningly.

'We'd better see what he wants,' said David, and

crossed the turf to where the man was standing. 'Yes? Do you want to see Professor Madison?'

The chauffeur looked relieved. 'Not exactly, although this would do,' he said, nodding. 'I have a message from Don Carlos d'Alvarez. It concerns the Señorita Madison.'

'Oh yes?' David frowned now. 'Well? What is it?'

The chauffeur held out a note, and David beckoned Carolyn forward. 'Here,' he said. 'It's for you.' The sarcasm in his voice was evident.

Carolyn opened the note wonderingly, her legs feeling like jelly. It was precise and to the point. *Señorita, I have been informed of your departure tomorrow morning. Knowing how unpleasant the journey is between here and Veracruz I am putting my helicopter and its pilot at your disposal. They will transport you to the nearest town of your choice and it will be a simple matter for you to gain transport to a suitable airport. I hope you will take advantage of this opportunity as a gesture of my thanks for your patience with Elena. Carlos d'Alvarez.*

She re-read the note disbelievingly, and then handed it to David. He read it, and raised his eyebrows sardonically. 'Well, well, well,' he said. 'He can't wait to despatch you, can he?'

Carolyn bent her head. 'Oh, don't, David.'

'I'm sorry.' He looked ashamed of himself. 'Well, at least that will save you a very hot and dusty journey.'

Carolyn stared at him. 'But I won't go.'

'What do you mean?'

'I mean, I shall go with Bill, as arranged.'

David gasped. 'You must be crazy!'

'Who is crazy, Laurence?' Professor Madison had

joined them, looking frowningly at the chauffeur. 'What is going on here, Carolyn?'

Carolyn handed him the note and he read it slowly. 'I see. Well, that is a good idea.' He turned to the chauffeur. 'You may tell your master that Miss Madison is pleased to accept!'

'*No!*' It was Carolyn who spoke. 'I shall go with Bill, as arranged.'

'But why, Carolyn? Ah, I see, this is what you were saying before when Laurence called you crazy. Well, for once I am inclined to agree with him. Of course you must accept the offer, and at least you will not require a complete change of clothes when you reach your destination. Besides, after all this rain the road is likely to be swampy in places. I would feel much more content if you were leaving in the helicopter.'

Carolyn looked mutinous. 'How did he find out I was leaving, anyway? I thought no one knew.'

The professor shrugged. 'I saw Ramon when I was at the hacienda only yesterday. Naturally I told him. I had not thought it was a secret.'

'It's not a secret, but—oh, Dad, I don't want to feel beholden to *him.*'

'What nonsense! You'll probably never see the man again. Yes, do as I asked, my man, tell Don Carlos my daughter would be pleased to accept his invitation. Now about transport to the airfield——'

'Er—Señor, I have been told to say that a car will collect the Señorita, in the morning.'

'Ah, good! Good! Very well, she will be ready.'

After the car had driven away, Carolyn turned and stormed into her tent, followed rather more slowly by her father.

'Carolyn, this is ridiculous. I will not have it! You would be all kinds of a fool to refuse his offer. Besides, you know perfectly well that you were very uncomfortable on the journey here.'

'I know, I know! It's just a feeling I have. I don't want to have to send a letter of thanks when I would much rather be in the Land-Rover.'

'I will do all the thanking that is necessary when I see him,' retorted her father impatiently. 'Now, for goodness' sake, let us have a few moments' sensible conversation before you go to sleep. We shall have no time in the morning, and we will all be gone to the dig before you leave. So, please, try and think of the good side of it.'

Carolyn sighed, but it was her last night, and she did love her father very much, and would miss him terribly, so she agreed at last, and the subject was dropped.

The next morning Carolyn breakfasted with the team, said her rather sad goodbyes to her father, and then slid her arms into the jacket of the linen trouser suit she was wearing. An attractive shade of coffee it complemented the creamy tan she had acquired, and she had wound her hair into a knot to keep it off her neck. Her father had hesitated at the last minute, wanting to go with her to the helicopter, but knowing how emotional she was likely to feel Carolyn begged him to let her go alone. She said she would write as soon as she reached England.

She waited impatiently for the car to arrive. It was already after nine thirty and the sun was getting hotter every minute. She paced about the encampment restlessly. Now that the time for departure had come she wanted to get away as quickly as possible.

At last the hum of an engine heralded the arrival of the vehicle, and she lifted her hand luggage in anticipation. The car stopped and she saw it was Ramon behind the wheel. She frowned, and when he got out, she said:

'What are you doing here, Ramon?'

He smiled, looking less fatigued than he had done before the smile broke up his taut features. 'I'm your chauffeur today,' he replied, calmly. 'Is this all your luggage?'

'Yes,' said Carolyn, thoughtfully, and then shrugging, she helped him stack the cases in the car. She slid into the passenger seat and waited for him to get in beside her. She was troubled that he should have come to collect her instead of the man of the night before, but she supposed she ought to feel grateful it was not Don Carlos himself, come to make certain she boarded the helicopter.

The hood of the car was down and a fresh breeze ruffled her hair, while the exotic scents of the flowers, which she had become so used to, were a constant reminder that soon she would leave all this warmth and beauty behind her. Her early impressions of the heat and the dust and the insects had given way to a genuine feeling for the valley, she suddenly realised, and she was struck again by the miserable prospect of taking up her now empty life in London.

The airfield was some distance from the hacienda, and although Carolyn had never seen it, Elena had told her it was possible to take off in a small light aircraft from it. Not that the aircraft was often used.

In the main the easier manipulated helicopter was more efficient. Carolyn was surprised to find that the airfield looked deserted, and the first faint twinges of doubt began to irritate her. It was irrational, and stupid, and yet she felt strangely disturbed, and she looked at Ramon thoughtfully, willing him to make some explanation and rid her mind of its perplexities.

As though aware of her preoccupation with her thoughts, he said: 'Do not be alarmed, Carolyn. The helicopter is over here, and the pilot will be along very shortly. I'll just start installing your cases.'

Carolyn shrugged, cast her doubts away, and helped him. The helicopter was big enough for three, a huge perspex observation cabin enabling its occupants to have a completely trouble-free view. She had never been in a helicopter before, and quite looked forward to the experience.

The cases installed, Ramon indicated that Carolyn should climb into the cockpit.

She hesitated now, her doubts becoming stronger. 'Ramon,' she began, awkwardly. 'Look, are you sure the pilot is coming?'

Ramon frowned. 'Of course. Don't you trust me?' The little hauteur on his part reminded her of his brother, and with a stifled exclamation, she climbed into the helicopter, looking down on Ramon who seemed to be avoiding her eyes. Then she inwardly chided herself for her ridiculous nervousness. It was all merely a reaction to that cool, businesslike letter Carlos had sent her. She felt about for her cigarettes, and lit one, moving over to the far side of the seat to see the lake below them more clearly. Every single detail of the valley seemed to be imprinted on her mind, never to be erased, and she sighed, wishing things could have been different.

She was startled into awareness of her situation when suddenly the propellers began to rotate, and the engine throbbed into life. Ramon had climbed in beside her, and because she had been so intent on the view she had not realised he intended to take off.

'*Ramon!*' she exclaimed, in astonishment. 'What are you doing?'

Ramon did not answer her and she turned and rattled helplessly at the sliding panel at the other side of the cabin. But she didn't know how to open it, and she gave up after a moment as the propellers rotated more swiftly and the helicopter gained a little elevation. She caught his arm, her eyes wide and frightened. But Ramon shook her off, concentrating on getting the craft off the ground.

Carolyn breathed swiftly shaking her head, unable to believe Ramon was doing this against her will. Deciding to remain calm, she said: 'Am I to understand you are taking me yourself?'

Ramon glanced her way momentarily. 'You can understand that, if you like,' he agreed, coolly. 'But we're not on our way to the airport, Carolyn.'

Carolyn pressed a hand to the fluttery feeling that was her stomach. 'Why?' she managed to ask.

'You must know why.'

'I don't, or I wouldn't be asking,' she cried.

Ramon shrugged, and as Carolyn looked down she saw the hacienda far below them. They were airborne. Well, she thought blankly, that at least had been accomplished, but what did Ramon intend to do now?

As though hearing her unspoken question, he said, relaxing a little: 'I suppose you are concerned as to why I should choose this method of—well, abducting you.'

'You could be right,' said Carolyn, dryly, feeling a little sick.

'Well, it's quite simple really. Carlos, and Manuel Costilho, cannot believe that I am serious when I say I love you, that I want to *marry* you. They continually treat me like a child who is unaware of his own mind. Believe me, they are wrong. I do love you, Carolyn, and I know that deep down you feel the same——'

'*No!*' she gasped.

'But, yes. Oh, I know you feel a responsibility towards Anna, and I must confess I do not like hurting her, but in something as important as this one should not concern oneself with the feelings of others.'

'Ramon, I don't love you!'

He merely ignored her, concentrating instead on a map which he had drawn out from a compartment in front of him. Carolyn felt completely impotent and stared out of the window blindly. In one thing Ramon was right; none of them had believed he had such a strength of mind, they had treated him like a child, and now she was having to pay for it.

'You realise the real pilot will tell your brother that the helicopter has disappeared, don't you?' Carolyn said, pleadingly.

Ramon gave a short laugh. 'Oh, Carolyn, you're so gullible! Mario said you read the note, all of you read the note, and not one of you doubted its authenticity!'

Carolyn's heart skipped a beat. 'You mean Carlos did

not write that note?'

'Carlos? Of course not. As far as I know he doesn't even know you're leaving the valley.'

Carolyn didn't know whether to laugh or cry. Allied to her fears now of what Ramon intended to do was the overwhelmingly sweet knowledge that Carlos did not know she was leaving, and that if he did find out he might conceivably care, just a little bit. Sufficient anyway not to send a note despatching her like an unwanted parcel.

'So this man—Mario—he was in league with you?'

'Of course.' Ramon laughed. 'It was so simple, really. We really pulled a terrific stunt, Carolyn.'

'*You* did,' said Carolyn, her elation fleeting as her unfounded optimism. 'Ramon, take me back, please. Or at least take me to the airport, where I'm expected to go.'

He shook his head. 'Carolyn, listen! You know as well as anyone how rigid and proper are Carlos's conventions. He demands the same discipline from us as he uses on himself. He is also unlikely to overlook our affair——'

'*Affair!*' she echoed, faintly.

'Yes, affair; as I was saying he is unlikely to overlook that if we have already anticipated our marriage by spending a night alone together.' When Carolyn gasped, he smiled, his eyes caressing. 'Don't tell me you haven't guessed that we're eloping!'

'*Eloping!*' Carolyn shook her head. 'Ramon, you're crazy!'

'No, not crazy, just madly in love with you,' he exclaimed, hotly.

Carolyn felt tired. 'Ramon, Ramon, understand

me,' she cried, desperately. 'I'm not joking, I'm not trying to placate your brother, I'm not even thinking of your fiancée, I'm only thinking of myself, and I *don't love you!*'

Ramon gnawed at his lip, the first traces of doubt appearing on his handsome face. 'You're trying to forestall me,' he said, at last. 'And I won't have it. Look, there is Hidalgo y Costilla, it is a very high mountain, is it not?'

Carolyn felt too confused to care, but she looked down and saw the valley of Zaracus was falling away to their right now, and they were crossing a range of mountains with hard, unyielding jagged peaks.

'Where are you going then?' she asked with resignation, unable to see any escape for herself, and only hoping she would be able to convince him of the recklessness of his actions when they were again on solid earth. Surely wherever they went there would be people and telephones.

Ramon studied the map on his knees more closely, and Carolyn stiffened as the helicopter seemed to falter as he changed course jerkily. Then he took the helicopter down, lower than before, so that Carolyn held her breath in complete petrification.

'Ramon,' she groaned, 'what are you doing?'

'You asked me where we were going,' he said, glancing her way. 'Now I can show you. See—these mountains form a natural boundary of the valley. They are not very high, but they are remote, and in the main uninhabited. However, there are huts there, used by climbers or peasants, and as I have food on board we will not starve. Tomorrow, we can return to Zaracus, and face Carlos with what we have done. I hardly think even he will raise any objections then.'

'Oh, Ramon! You're crazy,' she said again. 'You can't *land* in these mountains!'

'Of course I can,' he said, with a return of the hauteur she had noticed earlier. 'You may be interested to know that I am an experienced helicopter pilot, and were it otherwise I would not have used the craft. I am not stupid. I would not wish to take chances with our lives when we have so much to live for.'

Carolyn shook her head, gripping her seat tightly. It seemed completely foolhardy to her to try and set the helicopter down among boulders which could snap one of its blades like a piece of charcoal. But she knew it would do her no good whatsoever trying to argue with Ramon. He was so intent on destroying his brother's plans for him that he would not even listen.

The peaks seemed to be rushing up to meet them, but at last Carolyn could see the wider expanse of green which appeared to be where Ramon was making for. A small plateau, half-way up the mountainside, it seemed completely inaccessible from below, and was the ideal hideaway. She sighed. Of course, he would have thought of everything.

The helicopter hovered delicately, Ramon's whole attention absorbed by the task in hand. Carolyn closed her eyes. She didn't want to look. The craft came lower, and with shaking limbs she felt a faint thud which seemed to be earth below the helicopter. Her eyes swept open, and she ran a tongue over her dry lips. Ramon was holding the craft steady, not yet convinced of the security of his landing. Carolyn looked at him, seeing the tiny beads of sweat on his tanned brow, and feeling her own head found her hand came away wet. She had not been aware of the intensity of her tension.

Ramon bit hard on his lips. 'I don't think——' he began, and then: 'God! I was right,' as the helicopter tipped a little sideways.

'Ramon,' she gasped, clinging to her seat, but he shook his head impatiently, attempting to regain control of the craft. But the unsteadiness had unbalanced it, and it seemed to lurch forward, spinning off the ledge and plunging down several feet like a stone.

Carolyn felt sure they could never survive it. The helicopter was completely out of control now, and below the valley stretched deep and dangerous. The helicopter scraped violently along another ledge, while Ramon tried desperately to prevent its death plunge. A wall of rock seemed to loom up in front of them, and the last thoughts Carolyn had were that at least they were not to fall the several hundred feet into the valley. Then unconsciousness blessedly claimed her, and there was silence on the mountainside, only the wild call of the birds breaking the stillness.

## CHAPTER TEN

CAROLYN returned to consciousness slowly, unable at first to understand what had happened and why she should be half sitting, half lying on a hard, unyielding surface surrounded by the debris of the helicopter. Then it all came rushing back to her, the kidnapping, the flight and its implications, and finally the crash.

Putting her hand down to struggle up into a higher position she brought it swiftly back to her mouth, sucking it vigorously where some sharp material had pieced the skin of her palm. Her head throbbed violently, and she felt terribly sick. With an effort, she looked round, and saw Ramon, a crumpled heap below the control panel of the helicopter. Blood was oozing from a wound on his forehead, and he was still unconscious. She closed her eyes momentarily, willing away the feeling of faintness which suddenly engulfed her at the recognition of the hopelessness of their plight. She became aware that the sun which had been directly overhead when they crashed was now much lower in the sky, and although her watch was useless, broken in the impact, she knew it must be late in the afternoon and darkness would not be far away.

Knowledge of this and Ramon's difficulties brought her upright by pure strength of will-power, and she moved her legs and arms gingerly, half afraid of what she might find. She had felt numb from the waist down, and she had been afraid she might be paralysed in some way, but as she moved and blood flooded back into her limbs she was troubled only by an irritating feeling of pins and needles. She struggled to her feet, only to find she could not stand upright inside the fuselage. Grappling with the exit she remembered hers had been jammed earlier in the day, so she scrambled over the seat, past Ramon, and out through the broken door.

For a couple of minutes she stood transfixed, gazing about her in horror. Her feet had encountered turf outside the helicopter, but now she saw that she was standing on the edge of the ledge, and below a sheer drop of some sixty feet ended in yet another outcrop, thickly foliaged and yet ruggedly jagged with rock formations. She put an unsteady hand to her throat, unable to quell the surge of panic she now felt. Their situation was desperate, and as far as she could see completely hopeless.

Pushing these thoughts to the back of her mind, she turned back to Ramon. He had not stirred, and she shrugged out of the jacket of her trouser suit, pillowing his head with it. Then she explored the wound with gentle fingers. It was deep and uneven, and although it was not bleeding fast now, evidence that it had been doing so was all around him. Taking out her handkerchief she staunched the opening carefully, and then looked round for something with which to bind it in place. If only there had been some water, she could have bathed it, as it was she was afraid of the threat of infection.

Unable to find anything suitable she eventually found a safety pin with which to support her pants, and removed the belt from her waistband. Using this she managed to bind up the injury. Then she tried unsuccessfully to wake Ramon from his unconsciousness. But he didn't stir, or make a sound, and she felt terribly alone, and isolated. With his companionship their plight would have been bad enough, but with him unconscious beside her she could not dispel the fear which threatened to overwhelm her.

She was aware of a hollow feeling in the pit of her stomach, and she wondered how long it was since they left the airfield at Zaracus. She supposed she must be hungry, and yet she had no desire to eat anything. In truth, she felt sure that food would choke her. But she would have liked a drink, and so she searched among the pile of luggage behind the seats for the food which Ramon had said he had brought. Unfortunately, however, the flask Ramon had packed had been thrown out on impact and was broken completely. There was no sign of any wine or lemonade, and with a heavy sigh she sat back on her heels wondering what she could do. It was no use just sitting and hoping and waiting for someone to come and rescue them. They might not be missed jointly for days, and besides, who would expect to find them high up in these mountains?

Making sure Ramon was as comfortable as she could make him, she crawled out of the helicopter again to assess their position. Standing precariously beside the crashed machine she looked back, over the crumpled fuselage seeing that the ledge they were on went further into the wall of rock than she had first thought. They were on the edge and consequently she had imagined the ledge was much narrower than it really was. If she scrambled over the body of the craft she might be able to find some way of getting off the ledge and down the steep mountainside. It was no use thinking that such a task was an impossible one. There was nothing else for her to do, and only the throbbing in her head persisted in heightening her depression.

Making a final examination of Ramon she could see that he would not come round for some time yet. His breathing was shallow and swift, and she thought that his loss of blood might be considerably more dangerous than the bump he had received when the helicopter crashed. It was a mercy that they were both alive but she knew that if help was not brought soon Ramon could easily die there on the mountainside for after the sun had gone down it would be cold and chilling and all the time the blood was seeping out of him.

Standing terrified for a moment by the tortuous trend of her thoughts she had to force herself to turn away and attempt the climb over the craft.

The far side of the ledge revealed a narrower lip of rock running round the side of the mountain, and knowing that she could not wait any longer, Carolyn turned her face away from the hazardous drop below her and eased her way along the rock face. She had seen plenty of films back in England which made a great suspenseful incident out of the task she was trying to accomplish, and she felt an unwilling sense of hysteria rising in her at the knowledge that she was attempting to be a heroine when her knees were shaking and her palms were wet with sweat.

It seemed miles round the rock face. Every step she

took she expected to slip and fall, and when suddenly the rock gave inwards, she almost fell on to the grassy plateau she had now reached. She sank down on to her knees for a few minutes, getting her breath back, and recovering from her ordeal. She felt in her pocket but she had not brought her cigarettes and just now she would have loved one.

Shrugging her shoulders, she got determinedly to her feet and looked about her. The grassy plateau sloped more gently down the mountainside and she walked carefully to its edge. Below the plateau was more rock face, but she knew she had to go down sooner or later so it might as well be from here. Giving her hands a regretful glance, she turned and going down on her knees she let herself carefully over the ledge, searching desperately for a foothold. Finding one, she gripped an outcrop firmly before lowering herself a little further.

It was a slow, frightening business, her hands torn by the ridges, her clothes ripped and dirty. Her hair had come loose from its immaculate pleat, and hung in untidy ends about her shoulders. The sun was slowly sinking, and the air was becoming fresher, but she was so hot and sticky she didn't notice it.

Once she fell several feet, falling heavily on to a clump of broken bushes which saved her fall. She was bruised and she thought she passed out for a few minutes, as much from fear as injury, before continuing with her task. It got dark suddenly, and the sounds of the night were close around her. Once she thought she heard voices far below but she put it down to hallucinations, almost uncaring of what might happen to her.

The valley seemed to be coming no nearer although she had descended quite a long way, and she ached from head to toe. Her sandals, narrow-thonged and expensive, were broken and uncomfortable and only the knowledge that her feet would be cut to ribbons if she removed them prevented her from doing so. She thought about Carlos, and Louisa, and her father with a strange feeling of detachment, as though they were no longer part of her existence. Her mind seemed unable to assimilate the simplest things and once she found it hard to remember what she was doing here, and why.

Finally, her foot missed its way and she lost control of her fingers. Grappling and clawing for some kind of handhold, she slithered down the mountainside, not able to find the horror which she knew she ought to be feeling. Instead, she felt completely apart from herself, like someone else watching her body slide down the mountain. She wondered if she was dying, or was perhaps already dead, when her head struck a boulder and she knew no more.

When she came round again, the stars were brilliant above her, and a white moon illuminated the bare mountainside. She shivered, and then she heard voices, distinctly *voices*. She tried to struggle up, but her head throbbed too violently for that, and she lay there, helpless, wondering whether she was dreaming.

But no, again she heard them, speaking in a foreign language which for the life of her she could not identify. Then she concentrated hard, and realised it was Spanish. *Spanish!* Her heart pounded loudly.

Could it possibly be men from the villages, high up on the mountain passes? Or maybe climbers who had missed their way.

She swallowed, her throat parched and uncomfortable. Somehow, she must attract their attention, but how? If she couldn't move they would pass her by. She appeared to be lying in a small crevasse, invisible unless one was looking for it.

She moved her feet cautiously, feeling about for something on which she might be able to tap her foot. There was loose shingle, stones that rattled a little, but caused no more disturbance than the movement of a night creature, scuttling to its nest. Then her feet encountered a small boulder. It was loose, and with beads of sweat pearling on her brow she managed to move closer so that she could press both feet strongly against it. It moved, slowly at first, but then with increasing speed, and rattled away down the rocky face. She prayed no one was coming up in its path, and then relaxed, exhausted by the effort.

Lights were appearing, and for a moment she thought they were inside her head but they materialised as torches, powerful beams sweeping the terrain purposefully.

'Here,' she said, feebly, endeavouring to speak aloud. Her tongue seemed to cling to the roof of her mouth and it was not easy. 'Here!' she called again, this time more strongly, her throat aching with the effort.

Now there was noise and voices, coming closer, the accents pronounced, the tones excited. She tried to understand what they were saying but they spoke too fast and she was too weary.

One voice among all the rest was familiar, and she felt a strange stirring of excitement inside her, even though her body was one huge ache. It sounded like Carlos, but that could not be! He did not even know she was leaving, how could he be here, on the mountainside, searching for her?

With all her strength, she levered herself up on one elbow, and cried: 'Here I am! Down here, in the crevasse!'

The heavy foliage above her parted miraculously, and she stared disbelievingly into Carlos Fernandez Monterra d'Alvarez's dark face. '*Dios*, Carolyn,' he exclaimed, in a husky emotional voice, quite unlike his usual tones. 'We thought you were dead!'

Thrusting aside the men who had joined him, he stepped down purposefully into the crevasse, the knee-length boots only inches from her face. Then he bent, and ran his hands exploringly over her body, before finally lifting her bodily into his arms. He stood there for a moment, just looking at her, his eyes warm and concerned, and Carolyn buried her face in his neck, uncaring of the construction he might place on her action.

Suddenly, she remembered Ramon. 'The helicopter,' she began, and he shook his head.

'Do not concern youself, Carolyn. Ramon has been taken care of. It was you we were most anxious about. You have been missing for hours. We thought you must have fallen down the mountainside. We have been searching the lower slopes for a long time. We had almost given up hope when we heard your cry.' He was pale under the tan of his skin. '*En el nombre de cielo*, why did you not wait by the aircraft? I have been almost out of my mind these last few hours.'

Carolyn could hardly credit that this was the cold, aloof lord of Zaracus. His eyes burned with the evidence of his anxiety, while the body so close to her own trembled slightly as she stared at him.

Then, with a muttered exclamation, he brought her up, out of the crevasse, to where the rest of the party had a stretcher waiting to transport her down to the foothills.

The rest of the journey was a blur. All that Carolyn could think about was Carlos, and his obvious concern for herself, a concern moreover that was so out of character of the Carlos she had thought she knew.

A car was waiting to take them back to the hacienda, and Carolyn's father was sitting in the front seat. Carlos installed Carolyn on the back seat, and then slid into the driving seat himself.

'Carolyn!' Professor Madison looked shocked and anxious. 'My dear girl, are you all right?'

'I—I think so,' said Carolyn, faintly. 'What time is it?'

Carlos glanced at his watch. 'A little after three o'clock,' he said, shortly, and she shook her head in bewilderment, wincing as the movement caused a thundering in her temples. 'Three o'clock! Heavens, I didn't realise ...' Her voice trailed away.

Professor Madison gnawed at his pipe stem. 'That crazy young fool!' he muttered, looking angry. 'If he had not been so badly hurt himself I would have given him a piece of my mind.'

Carlos looked his way momentarily, and then concentrated on the dark road ahead. 'That will not be necessary,' he said, coldly. 'When Ramon has recovered I myself will deal with him!'

Carolyn heaved a sigh. 'Oh, please,' she said, unhappily. 'Be thankful we are both still alive. I am sure Ramon is sorry for what he did.'

Carlos did not look at her, but his tones were clipped. 'Just what had he in mind?' he asked, savagely. 'My God, I know I should not be asking these questions tonight, you've had a terrible ordeal, but I must know. Why did he take you in the helicopter?'

Carolyn swallowed hard. 'We—we were going to the—the airport,' she lied.

Carlos gave an angry exclamation. 'Do you expect me to believe that? After your father tells me that you received a note—purporting to be from myself—yesterday evening, advising you that I was offering you the use of the helicopter when I knew nothing about it?'

Carolyn closed her eyes. 'I expect Ramon did not wish to trouble you with it. Oh lord, my head aches!'

Carlos glanced over his shoulder, and his hands tightened on the wheel. Using the accelerator and his gears for easier braking, he gave the car its head, going as fast as he dared. 'Doctor Ramirez is at the hacienda waiting to see you.'

'At this hour of the morning?' she cried, weakly.

'Of course. He will be waiting for us to bring you back,' said Carlos, with the old arrogance returning. 'That is his job.'

Carolyn sighed, and let events take their course. So she was going to the hacienda again!

The events of the night became less clear. At the hacienda Carlos himself carried her inside, past wide-eyed servants, and up the stairs to a room she had not seen before but which she later learned was one of the guest-rooms. Then Doctor Ramirez was summoned, and a thorough examination was made before the doctor and Carlos departed to leave her to the ministrations of a curious Maria. The maid stripped her of her clothes, helped her into a warm, sweetly-scented bath, and then helped her to rid herself of all the dust and grime she had accumulated. Her hair was washed and dried by a warm-air heater, and finally she was dressed in a filmy nightgown which Maria told her was Señorita Rosa's. Her own cases had not yet been brought down from the wreckage. She questioned Maria tiredly about Ramon, but the girl seemed to know little except that the Señor had been in a flaming temper since he discovered their departure, and that none of the servants had been allowed to go to bed until she was found.

Carolyn apologised for the trouble she had caused but Maria merely smiled half curiously at her, and then went to tell the doctor that the Señorita was in bed. Doctor Ramirez brought her a glass of milk, explaining that a sedative had been put in it for her.

'Oh, but is that necessary?' asked Carolyn, shaking her head. 'I feel absolutely exhausted.'

'Of course. Unfortunately, the bump you have on your head may cause a little concussion and therefore a sedative will give you a more relaxed rest. I will be here to see you again tomorrow, or I should say later today.'

Carolyn managed a half smile before falling back upon the pillows, and then her face suffused with colour as Carlos himself entered behind the doctor, his features dark and saturnine in the muted lamps by the bed. Doctor Ramirez turned, and nodded his head, and then withdrew leaving them alone for a moment. She felt awkwardly conscious of the sheer quality of the nightgown and to draw the sheets closely around her would appear prudish. So she said, tightly:

'Th ... thank you, for everything!'

He moved closer to the bed, looking down at her intently. 'Thanks are not necessary,' he replied abruptly.

She allowed her teeth to catch her lower lip. She felt very tired and her eyes ached with the longing to close them. As though aware of this he clenched his fists, and said:

'I will have the truth, you know. I already have some of it, from Mario. What did Ramon think to do? Did he imagine that by abducting you he could force me to change my opinion about his request to marry you?'

Carolyn moved restlessly. 'Oh, not now, Carlos,' she whispered, a tear escaping from the corner of her eye, and rolling down her pale cheek.

He uttered an exclamation, going down on one knee beside the bed, taking her hand between both of his. Bending his head, he pressed his mouth to her palm, noticing the cuts and bruises with savagely disturbed eyes. Carolyn felt, tired as she was, the now familiar feeling of ecstasy his touch could bring. He looked up at her with passionate eyes, his gaze resting often on her mouth, as emotionally disturbing as a kiss.

'I will have you know that I do not intend that you should marry Ramon,' he muttered, violently, 'no matter what arguments you may present.'

'Carlos,' she began, slowly.

'No! Wait! I will make my commands known. Ramon may, or may not, marry Anna Costilho. This is a matter for him and his conscience, but whatever happens, he is not for you. Do you understand?'

Carolyn could scarcely take it in. 'I don't want to marry Ramon,' she protested weakly.

Carlos studied her for a heart-stirring moment, and then there was the sound of a door opening, and Carlos sprang to his feet as Louisa Morelos silently entered the room, her eyes going straight to the man who now stood so stiffly by the bed.

'Carlos?' she said, questioningly. 'What are you doing?' Her gaze shifted to Carolyn. 'Ah, I see, the Señorita is returned to us. How *delightful* for us all!'

Carolyn closed her eyes. 'Won't you please go?' she whispered, unable to stand any more tonight.

Carlos hesitated, as though he wanted to say more, but finally he allowed Louisa to take his arm and they left the room together. Carolyn heard the door close and then turned her face into the pillow, allowing the hot tears to pour unrestrainedly down her cheeks.

## CHAPTER ELEVEN

During the next two days she learned that Ramon had had to have several stitches in his scalp but his wound was healing satisfactorily. He had not asked to see her, but he had sent her a note, apologising for his behaviour, and she wondered whether Carlos had instigated such a thing. Of Carlos she saw nothing. She had half expected him to return when she awoke towards teatime the day following the accident, but he had not appeared, and she could only assume that some pressing business had taken him away from the hacienda.

Her father, who had left her to the doctor's ministrations the night of the accident, was a frequent visitor, much concerned about the pallor of her cheeks and the little they could persuade her to eat.

'For heaven's sake, child,' he exclaimed, 'you're losing weight lying here. As soon as you are fit again, we are going to London, both of us, and I will have a little holiday myself and try and put some life back into you.' He frowned, 'If I'd known this was going to happen I would never have let you come. I should have taken Don Carlos's advice and sent you home again.'

Carolyn did not answer, merely lying staring out of the window to the distant line of the hills. She had become listless, she knew it, but that was because she had misinterpreted a look, a touch, a kiss. She had mistaken normal anxiety for something much more and now she was completely without hope.

On the third day she was allowed to get out of bed, and sit by the window, looking down on the lake. Elena was allowed to visit with her, and later Rosa came. It was early evening when another tap came at her door, and when she called: 'Come in,' Louisa Morelos entered the room.

Carolyn stiffened. 'Yes,' she said, awkwardly. 'Can I help you?'

'Yes, Señorita, you can,' said Louisa, silkily. 'I want to talk to you.'

'I don't think there is anything to say between us,' said Carolyn, trying to summon up some energy to meet the other woman's maliciously narrowed eyes.

'Oh, but there is,' said Lousia, smiling. 'The last time we spoke together we were able to make things very clear between us. Unfortunately, Ramon's ridiculous sense of the dramatic has forced us back into the very situation I was trying to avoid.'

'I don't understand you, Señorita Morelos.'

'So you always say,' said Louisa. 'Unfortunately, I know otherwise. You see, I am a Spaniard, and as I am sure you are beginning to know a little about us you must also have realised that Carlos is not entirely indifferent to you—as a woman!'

Carolyn's cheeks burned, but she did not speak.

Louisa continued: 'So, because he is attracted to you, I think it is in your own interests to get as far away from here as possible, while you have time.'

'What do you mean?'

'I mean this, Señorita Madison. That Carlos is a

man, an intelligent man, with a man's desires and the—how shall I put it?—physical attributes to get what he wants when he wants it. If he wants you, do you honestly imagine you have a chance of preventing him? But do not let that heighten your hopes, Señorita. Carlos wants you like—well—any fine animal requires a mate——' She broke off abruptly as Carolyn's hand stung across her cheek. She almost spat out the rest of the words: 'You have realised the truth of it, Señorita, have you not? That is why you are so angry. Did you honestly imagine that Don Carlos Fernandez Monterra d'Alvarez could want anything more from *you*!' She laughed triumphantly. 'No, Señorita! When Don Carlos marries it will be to me, Louisa Consuelo Maria Teresa Morelos!'

'Get out of my room,' Carolyn said, tightly, 'before I throw you out!'

Louisa raised a dark eyebrow. 'Don't try to use your strong-arm methods on me, Señorita. You haven't the strength to throw out a mouse!'

But she went, just the same, leaving Carolyn a heaving, aching wreck upon the chair.

The night that followed seemed endless. Carolyn was unable to sleep, tortured by doubts and the certain knowledge that what Louisa had said was the truth. After all, hadn't Manuel Costilho said exactly the same thing?

She rose very early, and went to the balcony to stare out across the valley. Oh lord, she thought, if only I had gone with Bill, I would never have experienced any of this. If only Ramon hadn't interfered.

There was a tap at her door, and she spun round, a hand to her throat. 'Yes?' she said, shakily.

Elena entered, and Carolyn relaxed. 'Elena! What do you want?'

Elena closed the door. 'I wanted to see you, that's all. You haven't had much time for me since you came back.'

Carolyn had to smile. 'Honestly, Elena, I haven't had much time for anything. I—I've been exhausted.'

'I know. Ramon told me. He told me everything. Then I told Carlos. He was absolutely furious!'

'You told Carlos?'

'Yes. Of course.'

'But don't you know it's wrong to tell tales, Elena?'

'Of course. But sometimes—anyway, Carlos was in Ramon's room when I told him,' she replied defensively. 'He was threatening Ramon with all sorts of things, and Ramon was being sulky and saying he wasn't a small boy any longer, so I just told Carlos the truth. Then Ramon said it didn't matter any more because you had told him you didn't love him, and he was pretty sick of the whole affair.'

'I see.' Carolyn swallowed hard. 'When was this?'

'Yesterday, I think. Yes—it was.'

'Your brother—Carlos, that is—he hasn't been away?'

'No. No, he hasn't been away,' said Elena, in a puzzled voice. 'Why?'

'No reason,' Carolyn shook her head. 'Look, Elena, I want to leave here, today. But I want this to be a secret between us two. Do you think you could ask for a car for me, and not tell anyone else. If I can get back to the encampment, my father will be there and...' Her voice trailed away. 'Will you?'

Elena nodded her head vigorously. 'If that's what

you want,' she said, easily. 'When?'

Carolyn bit her lip. 'Why now, of course. Before anyone else is about.

'All right.' Elena slipped out of the room, and Carolyn hastily found some clothes. Most of her things had been recovered safely from the helicopter, but it would take too much time and trouble to take them with her now. She could send for them later. She dressed in a mustard-coloured linen skirt, and a green sweater, and fastened her hair back from her face with an elastic band. Then she took her handbag from its place by the table and left the room. The stairs were deserted, and she breathed a sigh of relief when she saw only Elena in the hall below.

'Is it fixed?' she whispered, conspiratorially.

Elena nodded, smiling, and said: 'Will I see you again?'

Carolyn sighed. 'Maybe, one day, who knows? Be good, Elena. Goodbye.'

Elena gave a wink, and turned back to the stairs. Carolyn opened the doors and walked out into the courtyard with its tinkling fountain. A lump came into her throat and she hastily turned the corner under the arch and came out into the road. The convertible was waiting for her, and she hurried towards it only to halt, uncertainly, when she saw who was at the wheel. Carlos slid out slowly, his eyes never leaving her face.

'*Dios*, Carolyn,' he said, huskily, 'you continually seem to be escaping from situations, or rather trying to escape from them. Unfortunately, this time, there is no escape!'

Carolyn's fingers clenched and unclenched round

the handle of the bag. 'Carlos,' she said, shaking her head, 'I don't know what you mean now. Please, let me go. I ought to have known Elena would find it exciting to do some more mischief——'

'*I* sent Elena to your room!'

'What?'

'That's right,' he said, calmly, walking lazily round the car towards her. Dressed in close-fitting charcoal trousers and a creamy-coloured sweater, open to reveal the darkness of his chest, he was disturbingly handsome. 'I knew you were awake. I had seen you at the window when I returned from my swim. I sent her to talk to you, to find out what your plans were. She told me.'

'So I see,' said Carolyn, shakily. 'However, that doesn't matter, Señor. I can drive. If you will give me the keys we can send the car back later.'

Carlos frowned. 'I have told you already, Carolyn, you are not going anywhere.'

Carolyn tensed herself. 'Aren't I? Then I shall just have to walk. Believe me, I will!'

She would have brushed past him but he caught her wrist, twisting her arm behind her back cruelly, bringing the tears to her eyes. She stared at him, almost hating him for humiliating her so, and then he bent his head and deliberately put his mouth to hers.

It was not like that other time he had kissed her when his whole desire had been to hurt, now his mouth was warm, yet insistent, gentle yet passionate, with an increasing pressure that caused him to release her arm to slide both his arms round her, pressing her body close against his. For only a moment she resisted, and then with a breathless gasp, she wound her arms round his neck and kissed him back.

The kissing lasted a long time. They were hungry for one another, and Carlos felt his iron control slipping at her unashamed response to his lovemaking. Then she seemed to come to her senses, and she said, brokenly:

'All right, Carlos, you've won. I won't leave. Just don't expect me to stay after you're married.'

'Married,' he murmured, caressing her neck with his lips. 'Of course you will stay. Where else would a wife be, than with her husband?'

'What!' Carolyn drew back from him, looking at him with unconcealed astonishment. 'Oh no, you don't mean this, Carlos. You're teasing me. Louisa told me——'

His expression darkened. 'I know exactly what Louisa told you,' he ground out savagely. 'However, Louisa will be leaving this morning with Manuel and Anna.'

'Leaving? Manuel and Anna, too?'

Carlos gave a wry smile. 'My darling Carolyn, how could I force my brother into a loveless marriage when I have just found that I cannot accept one myself?' He released her hair from its band, and buried his face in it. 'However,' he said a little thickly, 'our marriage must not be delayed. I find I am no longer in control of my emotions, but if you will agree to an early wedding I think I can wait.'

Carolyn was too bemused to believe it. 'But why? How?' she cried, not wanting to accept it until it had been proved entirely to her satisfaction. 'You haven't been near me for days!'

Carlos put an arm round her shoulders, and they

began to walk back to the hacienda. 'I will endeavour to explain,' he said, softly. 'When you came here I resented you. And why?' He smiled. 'Did you not know that love is akin to hate? I hated you because of what I saw in you—my lifelong standards of behaviour were being slowly and systematically destroyed by a girl not of my own race with sunlight in her hair, and green lakes in which to drown oneself for eyes.' He shook his head. 'I didn't want you, because for so long I had believed emotions could be moulded and subdued, to be taken out and used when necessary. You destroyed all this, and I tried to tell myself that you were wanton and permissive, when my hands longed to touch you, when my body longed to be close to you.'

Carolyn stared at him, her eyes warm and loving. 'You—you wouldn't believe a word I said, and I wasn't used to the kind of arrogance you display.'

'An unlikely situation,' he said, softly. 'The implacable object and the immovable force.'

Carolyn sighed, sliding an arm round him and feeling his swift response. 'Carlos,' she groaned, 'you won't change your mind?'

He allowed his mouth to trail across her face. 'No,' he muttered, huskily. 'I won't change my mind. The day you disappeared with Ramon I was frantic. We discovered you had gone almost immediately. Your father came up to the hacienda with some reports about the flooding and of course he thanked me for allowing you the use of the helicopter.' He closed his eyes, remembering that moment. 'Of course, I knew nothing about it, and when we discovered Ramon had disappeared it was not difficult to put two and two together. We found the wrecked helicopter some hours later when you had not landed at any of the immediate points and your father became worried.' He laughed mirthlessly. 'Not more so than I, believe me! A search was instigated and when I saw that crumpled mass I felt certain you were dead and that I had allowed the only good and sweet thing in my life to slip through my fingers.

'No one, not even Louisa, could have been in any doubt as to my true feelings at that moment. I had to get to you, to find you, to know whether my life was ended, or just beginning. When you were not with Ramon in the wreckage I was frantic.' He pressed her tightly against him. 'You can imagine my feelings. There seemed no way for you to have escaped.'

'I was trying to get help for Ramon,' said Carolyn. 'I didn't think anyone would miss us for hours.'

'So! Ah well, when we found you, so weak and drawn, I wanted to snatch you in my arms and make love to you, but again I had to be cautious. I had things to do. I was not yet free from Louisa. So I waited, and then I told her. It was only when I was coming to see you last evening that I inadvertently overheard part of her conversation with you. I questioned her when she left your room, and she admitted everything. What you did not know was that Louisa already knew that I loved you, that I needed you, and that I wanted to marry you.

'Afterwards, when I came back, I heard you crying. I could not come in then, it was too soon after Louisa. You would not have believed me. So I waited, I sat in the library all night, and this morning I sent Elena to your room. You see: I am completely at your mercy!'

'Oh, Carlos!' Carolyn pressed herself against him. 'You've no idea how I feel.'

'You do love me?' he asked, his eyes intent.

'Surely you cannot doubt that,' she murmured, her eyes wide. 'And I love the valley, and I want to stay here for the rest of my life.'

Carlos smiled: 'Which is just as well, as I do not intend that you should live anywhere else,' he replied, with a touch of his old arrogance.

# SAVE TIME, TROUBLE & MONEY!
## By joining the exciting NEW...

## Mills & Boon Romance CLUB

**WITH all these EXCLUSIVE BENEFITS for every member**

## NOTHING TO PAY! MEMBERSHIP IS FREE TO REGULAR READERS!

IMAGINE the *pleasure* and *security* of having ALL your favourite *Mills & Boon* romantic fiction delivered right to *your* home, absolutely POST FREE... straight off the press! No waiting! No more disappointments! All this PLUS all the latest news of *new books* and *top-selling authors* in your own monthly MAGAZINE... PLUS *regular* big CASH SAVINGS... PLUS lots of wonderful strictly-limited, *members-only* SPECIAL OFFERS! All these exclusive benefits can be yours – right NOW – simply by joining the exciting NEW *Mills & Boon* ROMANCE CLUB. Complete and post the coupon below for FREE full-colour leaflet. It costs nothing. HURRY!

*No obligation to join unless you wish!*

**FREE CLUB MAGAZINE** Packed with *advance* news of latest titles and authors

Exciting offers of **FREE BOOKS** For club members ONLY

Lots of fabulous **BARGAIN OFFERS** – many at **BIG CASH SAVINGS**

### FREE FULL-COLOUR LEAFLET!
**CUT OUT** CUT OUT COUPON BELOW AND POST IT TODAY!

---

To: MILLS & BOON READER SERVICE, P.O. Box No 236, Thornton Road, Croydon, Surrey CR9 3RU, England.
WITHOUT OBLIGATION to join, please send me FREE details of the exciting NEW **Mills & Boon** ROMANCE CLUB and of all the exclusive benefits of membership.

Please write in BLOCK LETTERS below

NAME (Mrs/Miss) ..................................................

ADDRESS ..................................................

CITY/TOWN ..................................................

COUNTY/COUNTRY .......................... POST/ZIP CODE ..........................

*Readers in South Africa and Zimbabwe please write to:*
*P.O. BOX 1872, Johannesburg, 2000. S. Africa*